Soul
Hoppers

A Short Novel

Laura Clementz

Disclaimer

This is a work of fiction. All the names, characters, businesses, places, events, and incidents in this book are either the product of the author's imagination or used in a fictitious manner. Any resemblance to actual persons, living or dead, or actual events is purely coincidental.

Laura Clementz
Bright Communications LLC
Cleveland, Ohio

Soul Hoppers
ISBN 979-8-218-31821-5

Chapter One

Cody joined the other catering staff gathered around a small but bulky television in the back of the kitchen. On the screen, a reporter sitting behind a news desk was looking into the camera with intensity.

"Hello. This is Andrea Saban from Era News. We have some breaking information. While there is no threat to our country of Kapra, there are confirmed reports of tanks and other military vehicles crossing the border into our neighboring country of Treaton. The troops are coming from the country of Atril who shares Treaton's eastern border." She paused. "As of yet, the Chancellor from Atril hasn't released a statement." Andrea covered her earpiece with her hand. "But, yes, we bring you Prime Minister Adamaris from Treaton, in a press conference already in progress."

The scene flashed to the Prime Minister, whose attire resembled a stiff military dress uniform. As always, his dark brown hair was brushed tight against his head. His lips were moving, but it took another couple of seconds for the sound to kick in.

"We all hoped for the best. We all prayed for peace as a country." The Prime Minister looked down at the podium in silence for a breath. "However, we were wise to prepare for the worst. As you know, our troops were on alert and are already moving into position to protect the capital and our port city of Ecrad." This time he looked forward while broadening his chest.

"We are all in this together. Together we will prevail."

As he continued speaking, both of his hands moved in tune with his words. "Let's pray for triumph over the tyrants who claim parts of this land were wrongly taken from them so many generations ago." He let his hands rest on the podium. "Thank you." He nodded to each side of the room.

The room erupted with chatter from reporters begging to have their questions fielded, yet Prime Minister Adamaris wouldn't give the concrete answers they craved.

Cody lost his remaining focus on the news broadcast when he heard a familiar voice. "Hey, let's get out of here for our own drink before the party gets started."

"Yah, let's go." Cody turned and walked along with Micka. They zigged-zagged through a few hallways to reach an unobtrusive exit off the side of the mansion.

As they got outside, Micka looked upwards scanning the towering brick walls and arched windows touched by the colors in the sunset. "Man, this place is over the top."

"For sure." Cody inspected the immaculate grounds and smelled the coastal breeze before accepting the flask Micka handed him. "From the looks of things, it must be the Whitmore's anniversary party tonight. You know, this is the third time I've been here, and I don't even know who Mr. Whitmore is." He raised the flask to his lips.

"I think his name is Darian. Darian Whitmore. That sounds right." Micka took the flask back into his grasp. "I was there during his introductions a couple of times. He looks like he's all scrunched up."

"Scrunched up?" Cody tilted forward and laughed.

"Yah." Micka walked around with his shoulders hunched over and sinking at the hips. "He's got a round belly and serious man boob potential." He stumbled a step backwards and smiled. "Someone needs to stretch him out like taffy."

"Oh man, don't go there." Cody laughed again. "At least he lets us have the leftovers. The shrimp and those mini beef wellingtons…" He leaned back and patted his stomach. "Hey, make sure to fill your flask. We'll have a feast tonight."

"You're on." Micka raised his flask, then tucked it away in his breast pocket.

"I couldn't imagine living like this guy does, having the finest of everything. Drinks served poolside all day and lavish parties at night. Bet his wife isn't half bad either." Cody tilted his head back and looked at the sky. "What a life!"

"Sure, but I figure it's not all that it's cracked up to be."

"Suit yourself. I'll take it any day. I can almost taste the sweet pleasure." Cody brought his thumb and adjoining fingers together and raised them to his lips for a chef's kiss. Then he walked with his friend back to the kitchen.

~~~

Josephine picked up the pen and signed the revised last will and testament. After the last stroke, she slid the paper across the coffee table in the quaint sitting room of the suite at the inn.

Her lawyer nodded. "Very well. Your sister will remain as the Executor, but this will leave most of your assets to Ella Turner." He pulled another piece of paper out of his leather satchel. "This is an additional affidavit stating that, to your knowledge, Ella is unaware of your estate planning."

Josephine accepted the document and produced another signature. "Yes, of course. We wouldn't want a supposed conflict of interest between a board member and executive director to make matters more complicated."

The lawyer took the document and handed it to the notary public sitting by his side. "It's just precautionary."

Josephine set the pen on the table. "Such a shame it has to be so complicated. Ella and I have known each other for years and, these days, she helps take care of me."

The notary finished making the documents official and organized the papers into a neat stack.

The lawyer took over the stack and stood, putting everything into his satchel with care. "I'm sorry that we must leave right away. It's always a pleasure visiting you."

"Thank you for meeting me on such short notice. I didn't know I would be in town, but SecondHope needs to prepare in case refugees come across the border from Treaton." Josephine rose from the sofa with effort. She used one hand to brace herself and increase her grace.

"Josephine, you are a saint." The lawyer extended his elbow as they walked towards the door of the suite.

"Oh, you know." She wrapped her wrinkled hand around the crook of his arm. "Everyone deserves a second chance." She let out a small chuckle. "Goodness knows, I've had many." At the doorway, Josephine exchanged his elbow with the doorframe to steady herself.

Just then Ella appeared from her adjoining room. She looked regal in her floor length evening gown. The French blue brought out the blue flecks in her eyes and accented her short, sandy-blonde hair. With elegance, she added her farewell to the departing lawyer and notary. "What was that all about?" she asked.

"It was nothing. Just some business." Josephine turned towards her room and lost her balance for a step.

Ella reached to steady her. "Where's your cane? You know you should use it."

"I don't want the damn cane." Josephine kept moving down the hallway. "Just let me get my shawl and we'll be on our way." She disappeared into her room, but her voice lingered. "We don't want to keep the Whitmores waiting."

~~~

By the time Cody started serving hors d'oeuvres in the dining hall, guests were already mingling in transient groups. Their elegant attire accented the surroundings where the tables were covered with crisp ivory linen set with china showcasing delicate patterns. Cody circulated with his tray while maintaining exceptional form and using all the right words. He kept a steady expression enhanced by an occasional charming smile. It also didn't hurt that he was dark-haired and looked extra handsome in the catering uniform that included a black classic bowtie and vest. He had reached the far end of the room when a harpist started to play. The tray, now depleted, sent Cody back to the kitchen where he exchanged it for another filled with delicate salmon canapés topped with fresh dill.

A few steps back in the dining area, he felt a subtle weight on his right side. It was as if he had a wooly blanket on his shoulder that was trailing down to his arm. He turned in that direction and met eyes with an old woman who was staring at him. Her eyes, surrounded by aged skin, glistened with a greenish hue that penetrated into his very being.

A guest reaching for a canapé brought him back into focus, but as soon as he served them, he looked at the old woman again. She was still staring straight at him. He had every impulse to cross the room and settle into the empty chair by her side. *What is this all about? She's like a million years old.*

Cody felt his shoulders wriggle with a chill as the old woman whispered something to the younger woman standing next to her. The younger woman nodded and started walking in Cody's direction. As she approached, he looked up and down the length of her body. *Now that's more like it.*

When he realized there was a grin on his lips, he jerked his head downward and gave it a small shake.

"Excuse me? Are those salmon canapés?" the younger woman asked.

"Yes, would you like one?" Cody noticed that despite her form-fitting gown, she had a soft voice and air of naivety.

"Oh no, but they are Josephine's favorite. Would you mind taking them over to her?" She gestured towards the older woman with the glistening eyes.

"Not at all." He turned in Josephine's direction, but all he could do was stand and stare.

"Don't worry. Josephine has that effect on some people." With a soft touch, the woman placed her hand on Cody's shoulder. "She's devoted her life to giving to others."

Cody nodded and walked over to the table.

"Ma'am, the young lady said you might like an hors d'oeuvre." Cody offered the tray and Josephine set a canapé on her plate with surprising elegance. Even in the dim light of the dining hall, the tiny sparkles in her chiffon dress glistened with her slightest movement.

"The woman's name is Ella. And she is, among many things, the executive director of my organization." Josephine grinned for a moment. "Do I know you? It seems we have met."

"No, ma'am. Not that I can recall."

"Oh, don't ma'am me. I insist you call me Josephine." She patted the seat of the chair next to her. "Here, come sit for a minute. Tell me about yourself. I won't be mingling tonight."

It seemed natural; his body moved to take the seat, but he caught himself in a flinch. He took a small step back. "No, I couldn't."

"I suppose not." She used her fork and knife to cut the hors d'oeuvre in half and said, "Maybe some other time."

"Of course." Cody headed back to the kitchen and didn't notice his speed increased the closer he got to the swinging door. Micka followed him in and pulled him to the side.

"Hey, what's the rush? You look like you're buggin out."

"There's this old woman and her eyes…" Cody rubbed his forehead.

Micka slapped Cody's back and laughed. "Man, you know, those older women can be very persuasive in seeking young companionship."

"It wasn't like that. At least, I don't think it was." He looked at Micka. "It was more like I've known her *forever*."

Chapter Two

The anniversary party rolled on and the main course, followed by dessert with coffee, was a smooth success. The house staff cleaned up the dining room while the caterers packed their equipment. Everyone reconvened towards the back of the kitchen where they had arranged the remaining food out on the counter. They filled their plates and filled the room with chatter mixed with quiet laughter. Cody joined in on the laughter but didn't talk that much. Instead, he stretched out his legs and took in the flavor of each bite from his plate and savored the smoothness of each swig from Micka's flask.

Soon, the group dispersed, and a few people started cleaning off the counter. He smiled to himself while walking over to where the kitchen manager was bustling around. "Hey, what can I do?" he asked.

"Here. Take these over to the double-door refrigerator in the main kitchen and put them on the middle shelf." She handed him a carton of milk and a small cheese tray.

"I can see why you're in charge around here." Cody took the items and walked to the far wall of the kitchen. Turning down the adjacent walkway, he was surprised to see the refrigerator door open. He wondered if someone left it open by mistake, but soon he wondered if there was someone's hand wrapped around the handle. In a few more steps, his brow crinkled. The hand had stubby fingers that were tapping on the stainless steel. Cody moved his head to the side, trying to see more of the person. The door closed part way and a stalky man with dark matted hair looked at him.

Cody gestured his chin in the refrigerator's direction. "Apologies. I was just putting away a few things."

The man let the refrigerator door swing open and took a step to the side while adjusting his robe around his thick waist. "I didn't know anyone was still around here."

Cody walked to the other side of the open door, then stopped. Darian Whitmore was just as Mika described. "Mr. Whitmore, sir?"

"Yes." Darian slid his hands into the pockets of his robe.

"Is there anything I can get for you?"

"Yes. I was looking for my seltzer water. Where the hell is it?"

"Let me retrieve you a bottle right away. It's probably in the back." Cody shifted to set the milk and cheese tray on a nearby counter. As he watched his hands release their grip, something took over. Or rather, his mind folded back into itself and went to the place where there are no thoughts, yet everything is known. The mere second when he could shake himself out of the progression was upon him. He turned and looked at Mr. Whitmore. "If you don't mind, I need to get by you."

"Sure, sure." Mr. Whitmore stepped to the side. "Get on with it already."

Cody looked down and took deliberate steps towards the refrigerator and closer to Mr. Whitmore. His foot planted next to the billionaire when, in a swift motion, he shifted to the side and pushed Mr. Whitmore against the closed freezer door. Raw surprise and fear seemed to keep the man from yelling out. Then Cody wrapped one hand behind the man's neck and placed the other over the man's heart.

Mr. Whitmore jerked his body back and used his hands to grasp at Cody's wrists in an attempt to free himself. Cody used all his strength to drag the struggling man towards the open refrigerator. They banged into the refrigerator door and it rattled in protest. But now that the man was trapped, Cody took the opportunity to get closer to him. The closer they were, the better.

Mr. Whitmore continued to grasp and growl until his face turned red. Like a boa constrictor, Cody held fast until the man's hands slowed and his grip weakened. The growls faded. The trance was taking hold.

"Shhh… Shhh… It will be over soon. I promise. Do your best to be calm," Cody whispered.

Cody bent his head forward and touched foreheads with Mr. Whitmore. It only took a few seconds before streaks of different colored lights filled Cody's peripheral vision. The colored streaks drew in until they took over his world. It felt like he was underwater, with every color of light dancing around him. He floated along and the colors joined together at a single point just in front of him. Where the colors joined, they created a white light. A small point at first, then growing larger.

Something inside Cody knew he had to let go and give himself completely. He had the knowledge that souls embody consciousness and they are indeed ethereal. But souls are also gelatinous. Like thick oil, they mix only when stirred, yet always leave a residue, a bit of themselves behind. The only time mixing is good is when they return to The Origin, and in that way, a soul is occasionally able to become one with all things.

As the white light grew larger, it breathed with its own life, expanding and contracting until it took over the entirety of Cody's vision. Then the white light spun and closed in around him while the base of what would be his stomach dropped. The sinking sensation transitioned to feeling tight and orgasmic before it shifted inward and traveled all the way up to his head. Now his soul would be in Darian's body and, as far as he knew, Darian's soul would be on its way back to The Origin. On its way home.

In an instant, his eyesight returned to the physical world. He watched Cody's lifeless frame, with the handsome face and dark hair he had styled earlier that day, thump onto the floor.

I guess you can call me Darian. He chuckled out loud and stepped over the body. With a quick inspection of his new body, he found he could see and feel the weight of his stomach. And his back ached. He shook his head. *This body's disgusting, but I'll be sleeping on clean sheets, next to my lovely wife, in a mansion tonight.*

Darian went over to the counter and grabbed the carton of milk the caterer was supposed to put away. He opened it before tossing it next to the body. The milk streamed out onto the floor as he yelled, "Hey, someone help! Now." With quick steps toward the staff area, he said, "This kid just collapsed by the refrigerator. Call an ambulance." He came around the corner and looked at the kitchen manager. "Did you hear me?"

But she was already standing with the receiver of the phone next to her ear.

Darian opened the front door just as the Roseacre Police came barreling up the drive, followed by two ambulances. Bright lights swirled that sent red and blue colors across the yard. Two male officers approached as the ambulance crew was pulling a stretcher out of the vehicle.

"Yes, he's in here. Hurry." Darian tried to produce an authoritative growl. "The kid seemed fine. Then he just went and collapsed on my kitchen floor."

"Yes, sir," the officer with blond hair said while the shorter officer with dark hair waved the ambulance crew forward. Two men dressed in paramedic uniforms carried a stretcher and dashed up the steps before releasing the wheels to the ground.

Darian turned and led the way to the kitchen. "I don't think he's a…" he trailed off.

"Alive?" the dark-haired officer asked.

"Yah, alive." Darian took a few more steps. "We're almost there."

Once Darian reached the far side of the kitchen, he used his arm to direct the paramedics down the way. He couldn't look at the body again. He was ready to move on with his new life.

The officer with blonde hair followed the paramedics while the officer with darker hair stayed close to Darian. "I'm Officer Dusky with Roseacre police. I wish we were meeting under different circumstances." He pulled a leather-bound pad and pen out of his breast pocket. "Is there somewhere we can talk? I need to get your account of what happened."

"Oh. Yes." Darian guided the officer. He noticed a room that looked like a lounge on the way down the hall. "We can sit in the parlor."

The two men got comfortable in the ornate room, and Dusky's questioning went as Darian expected. He had been in many bodies and had been through this a couple of times. It was even easy to surmise they would find the caterer died from an undiagnosed heart condition. Besides, this time he was a predominate rich man in a lily-white world. This will be easy.

"Dear, are you okay? What's going on?" A woman in a long cream night gown and matching silk robe that seemed to float around her walked into the parlor. She got closer and put a hand on her chest. "Thank goodness I found you. For a second I thought…" She pointed towards the kitchen, then covered her mouth before speaking again. "For a second I thought it was you laying on the kitchen floor."

That's my cue. It must be my lovely wife. Darian took a few seconds to skim his eyes up and down the curves of her pleasing body. Then he noticed the smoothness of her face, the brightness of her eyes, and the glimmer of her blonde hair. He stood and stepped to her side. Not sure what to do, he put a hand on her shoulder. She fell into his chest and he said, "There. There. I'm fine. Something happened to one of the caterers." He rubbed her shoulder.

Once his words faded into the air, she shifted and put her arms around him. Then rested her chin on his shoulder. "I don't know what I would do without you," she whispered.

He pulled back and examined her expression. Without darting her stare around the room, she still looked like a scared fawn looking for its mother. "Oh, now. Let's talk about this later," he said in a hushed but abrupt tone before turning towards the officer. "Are we done here? It's been a long night."

Dusky flipped his notepad closed. "Yes, I have all that I need for the moment." He returned the pad and pen to his pocket and rose from his chair. "Thank you, Mr. Whitmore. I'm sorry your celebration ended in such a way." He shifted his large frame to step by the couple and slip out the door.

Darian walked with his wife into the upstairs bedroom. He paused in the doorway to absorb his surroundings. It was a vast room with large arched windows to match. In between two windows was an entranceway to a full sized balcony that overlooked the sea. With only the screen doors open, the sound of crashing waves and the smell of seawater were part of the room as much as anything else. The ceiling to floor window sheers caught in the breeze caressed a chair in a living room suite that was arranged in front of the balcony. Across the room lay a king-sized bed with large pillars on all four corners supported by an ornate headboard and footboard.

His wife continued to a doorway across from the bed. Darian noted it was a bathroom as she stepped inside and closed the door. Alone in the room, the urgency to find out her name caught up with the rest of his mind. He walked over to a large desk in the nearest corner of the room and scanned the desktop. The edges of his mouth pulled up in a grin when he spied a copy of the invitation from the party that night. It read, *This invitation is to invite you to celebrate the Tenth Anniversary of Darian and Grace Whitmore…*

While repeating Grace's name in his head over and over, Darian's eyes wandered across the surface of the desk to look for more information. There didn't seem to be anything revealing, but a brochure for a psychic medium amused him for a second. A thump emanated from the bathroom. He craned his head in that direction, but the bathroom door stayed closed.

As his eyes wandered back to the desktop, he didn't miss the small bar across from the sitting area. Next thing he knew, he had a heavy crystal glass in his hand and was filling it with ice. He knew the type of alcohol by the color that shone through the elongated etched decanters. *A little scotch over ice sounds nice.*

With the drink in his hand and the ice clicking in the glass, Darian walked by the loveseat in the sitting area. His free hand found its way onto the seat cushions and as he moved down its length, his fingertips roamed its feel. Then he walked in between the flowing curtains and stepped out onto the balcony. Reaching the stone railing, he set his drink on the ledge and looked around. In the dark, he scanned the small white tips gliding in on the breaking waves and let them become part of his being. From the second story view of the impenetrable stone mansion, he felt the entire sea was at his feet. He picked up the glass and raised it in the air before bringing the drink to his lips. When he took a swallow of the fine liquor, he caught sight of a swift cloud floating across a bright full moon.

Darian jumped in reaction to the sound of Grace's voice. "What are you doing? It's so late."

He looked in her direction. "I was just having a nightcap and soaking in the view." His eyes returned to the water. "Something about watching that caterer collapse. It's staying with me."

"That's understandable." Grace took a step closer. "But let's go to bed. Get some rest."

Still feeling empowered by everything, Darian leaned back and let go of a satisfying laugh before saying, "Yes, Grace, let's turn in for the night."

Expressionless, she stared at him for a couple of heartbeats before heading back into the bedroom.

Darian waited on the balcony for a sign that Grace had settled into bed. He had to find out on which side he slept. After a moment, the light coming from the inside dimmed. His steps slowed as he entered the room, then he pulled the balcony doors part way closed before sliding into bed. The fine white sheets billowed before resting on his legs while his head fell onto the down pillow. He nestled into the softness with an enormous smile stretched across his lips.

Grace turned partway towards him. "Good night."

He patted her hip and searched around his insides for the residue of the previous soul to get a sense of their good night ritual. "Yah, night babe," he said and settled deeper into the mattress. Even though it was their anniversary, he knew this wasn't the right time to heat up the bedroom.

Chapter Three

Darian opened his eyes after the deepest night's sleep he'd had in years. Still disoriented, he propped himself on his elbows and looked around the room. He heard a hairdryer in the bathroom and the events from the previous day flowed into his mind like water. His wife, Grace, was beautifying herself for the day ahead. He twisted to the side and kept his eyes on the bathroom door. The sound of static and a male voice came from the bedside table. "Good morning, Mr. Whitmore. Will you be down for breakfast soon, or should we send it up?"

Darian looked at the intercom station and pushed the talk button. "Send it up. We'll be having breakfast on the balcony today." He let go of the button and chuckled. On a second thought, he pushed the button again. "Hey. What's on my schedule for today?"

After a momentary pause, the response came, "I'm not sure, sir. I'll have Tildy contact you."

"Good. And make is snappy," Darian barked into the speaker. He put his hands behind his head and leaned back into the pillows. Memories from his life as a caterer spun into his head along with memories from lives further past and he knew someone like Mr. Whitmore wouldn't give the staff the time of day, let alone be kind to any of them.

Grace emerged from the bathroom. Her make-up was flawless, and her clothes screamed of expensive and refined elegance. Darian watched her as she walked across the room. Just out of the shower, she radiated an intoxicating floral smell. *Anyone would be crazy to pass on her.*

The intercom system came to life again, this time with a female voice he assumed was Tildy. "Hello, Mr. Whitmore. How can I help you this morning?"

Still focused on his wife, he hit the button. "Do I have to say it again? What is on my schedule for today?"

"No, of course not, sir. You have a 10:00 with Baker & Ganovich and…" Tildy continued, but Darian barely processed a word until his ears tuned in to what he considered important. "…Officer Dusky wanted to talk to you, so I scheduled him in for 1:00."

"Cancel it all. Clear my day." He let go of the talk button for a second. "But tell Dusky he can come by anytime he wants. I'll be spending the day here."

"Will there be anything else?"

"Yes, I want services and lunch by the outside pool. And, wait, hold on a minute." He let go of the button and turned in Grace's direction. "Let's have dinner at the house tonight. It's a shame our anniversary night was interrupted."

"Oh, uh, sure. We could eat in the conservatory." Grace picked up a small designer handbag. "You enjoy having dinner there."

Darian turned his attention to the intercom again. "Yes. And arrange for dinner with all of Grace's favorite dishes in the conservatory." He grinned at his wife.

Grace scanned his body before meeting his eyes and he thought he saw it again. A wisp of fear in her eyes. She nodded and went back to putting make-up in the handbag.

When Darian stood as he got out of bed, his back protested while the extra weight on his body made him feel off balance. "God!" He stretched his shoulders upward to stand up straight. "I'm gonna start working out. Today."

"Well, the doctor suggested you get a trainer."

Darian trotted over and pulled Grace into a closed dancing position. He knew there was nothing sexier than a man who could change. "Of course, dear. I'll start with swimming some light laps until a suitable trainer can be found."

She laughed. "You? Swimming laps? That's new."

He guided her through a few dance steps. "Oh, you think that's funny? Well, there are still a few things you don't know about me."

"I doubt that," Grace said in a flat tone. She released herself from his grasp to answer a knock on the bedroom door.

A tall young man in a full uniform pushed a cart into the room. His medium-brown hair was styled in a fashionable bowl cut that somehow complemented his perfect posture. "Good morning. Breakfast on the balcony, correct?"

"Yes, and it's about time," Darian replied.

Grace released a breath and walked over to the balcony. She watched the attendant finish arranging the plates and food. "Thanks, Henry. That will be all," she said, and offered him a smile on his way out the door.

Darian walked to the balcony, a hand on his lower back the entire time. He sat down to the elaborate breakfast and his nose helped his eyes anticipate the variety of flavors before him. "Are you coming to have breakfast?"

Grace took a step onto the balcony but left one hand on the door frame. "I'm having an early lunch with Josephine."

"Josephine?" Darian tapped into his last memories as the caterer. "You mean the old woman?"

Grace took a step closer and flopped her hands to her side. "Yes, I guess. The old woman." She pulled her hands up to her hips. "She's worried about helping the refugees coming across the border from Treaton. Maybe we should offer to have a fundraiser?"

Darian didn't like the thought of seeing the old woman with glistening eyes again. He calculated further. It helped that Josephine wouldn't recognize him in his new body. And this could be an opportunity to make some headway with Grace. He met eyes with his wife. "Sounds good." He waved a hand in the water's direction. "If you want, we could have a dinner party on the terrace and charge ridiculous amounts for a plate. It would be grand."

"Are you certain?"

"Yah, sure. Somebody has to help at the border and it isn't going to be me." He took his first bite of scrambled eggs seasoned with expert precision and closed his eyes to relish the taste.

~~~

As the car pulled up to the inn, Josephine smiled despite the rain showers falling on downtown Roseacre. It was an enjoyable lunch with Grace. On top of that, Grace's generous offer was the security she needed to feel at peace.

Ella greeted her at the door of the suite and held it open until she navigated her way inside.

"How was your lunch?" Ella asked.

"Spectacular." Josephine had resigned to using the cane while she walked across the sitting room. She let her body rest on the seat of the sofa.

Ella picked up the remote for the television. "Let me turn this off."

"No, no." Josephine raised a hand. "It's the news."

Ella turned up the volume. On the screen, the news introduction ended and a reporter at the desk appeared. "Hello, I'm Andrea Saban from Era News. So glad you're with us this afternoon. At the top of the news, the troops from Atril are closing in on the Treatonian capital of Mightwell." She paused while looking into the camera. "We go now to Warren Reuel, who is in the field. Any updates for us, Warren?"

The scene flashed to a reporter wearing a green anorak jacket while standing in the middle of Mightwell's large town square. In the background were stone buildings that bore bold architecture. The reporter was silent for a few seconds before saying, "Yah, so far, there has been no fighting in the area. But if you look to the side of me…" There was a pause as the camera panned towards the east. "There are barricades of sandbags with military vehicles and armed soldiers ready to defend the capital." He leaned into the camera's view and gestured in that direction. "I've been told this is only the first of three barricades that extend outwards from the city." The camera panned back to Warren's face. "Reports from the other side of town are that they have established a safe corridor for citizens who are evacuating to Kapra." A breeze picked up and blew his hair away from his forehead. "Yet all this may be in vain if the Atrilian troops take a surprise turn to the south to capture the city of Ecrad. The port city, a vital part of the shipping industry and the location of Atrilian spiritual sites, has had the two countries at odds for centuries." He placed a hand over his earpiece and nodded. "This is Warren Reuel reporting from Mightwell. Back to you, Andrea."

Josephine shifted her body in Ella's direction. "It's time to return to Dewcall. The refugees will come across through our shared city."

"Yes, Frank called about an hour ago. Chef is preparing to start food service just outside the train station and Frank will transport those in need to our facility." Ella sat down next to Josephine. "Are you sure you are up to traveling that far?"

"It'll be fine, you'll see." Josephine let silence fill the room. "Grace must have worked some kind of magic on Darian. The Whitmores offered to host a charity event."

"That's wonderful." Ella clasped her hands together. "The funding will go such a long way."

"Yes." Josephine returned Ella's growing smile before she used the cane to rise from the sofa. "It's been a long couple of days. I want to get some rest before dinner." She could feel Ella's eyes as they studied her movements.

"I'll bring in your medications in a few minutes," Ella said.

Josephine paused before taking another step. "You're such a dear."

Just as Josephine got settled into bed, she heard a soft knock on her door. Ella approached the bed with a small tray to carry bottles of medications and a glass of water. She set the tray on the nightstand with the lamp, then pulled up a chair. "Here we are…" She picked-up a bottle and unscrewed the lid.

Josephine placed a hand on her arm. "Would you hand me the water first? I need a drink."

"Of course." Ella moved her hands to the water glass, which she passed into Josephine's frail grasp.

Josephine sat up in the bed to take a sip. "Don't worry about the pills just yet." She took another sip and closed her eyes for a moment. Her mind turned inward on itself and her thoughts disappeared. She was ready.

In a slow, steady motion, Josephine leaned over and placed the glass back on the nightstand. Situating herself back into the pillows, she gestured with her hand. "Come closer, dear."

Ella wrinkled her forehead but leaned forward. "What is it?"

Josephine put a hand over her own chest. "I just wanted to thank from my heart." She moved her hand from her chest to let it rest over Ella's heart. "To yours."

"That's very kind, but you don't have to thank me. We've become friends."

Josephine locked eyes with Ella. "Yes, we have." She placed her other hand on Ella's shoulder and nudged her closer until she could slide her hand around the back of Ella's neck. "We have accomplished so much together," she whispered.

Josephine understood the trust and admiration Ella bestowed upon her. It was that type of trust and admiration that took Ella into the trance with ease. With a tilt of her head forward, Josephine met her forehead with Ella's. Colored lights filled her peripheral vision. The colors danced as they overlapped and separated in a rhythm that has always existed. In their dance, they created a single white light that lay before Josephine.

As the white light grew, she felt the heaviness of her body disappear and she gave her entire self to the process, just as she had many times before. As the white light enclosed her in its pulsating embrace, she meditated on the feeling of being in that space. It was the only space she knew that must be like returning to The Origin. For less than a brief second, it would reveal the secrets of being able to leave the world and become one with all things. The secrets to ending the tormenting cycle of birth and death. Until she somehow embraced those secrets, she would accept having to move from body-to-body and the sacrifices involved in giving herself to others the same way she gave herself to the white light. The white light surrounded her and spun as it met with her inner essence. This time, at the last second, she felt it. A small spark that entered what would be the base of her spine and the energy streaked up her body until it seemed to burst out of the top of her head. The exchange had taken place.

Her eyesight returned to the world around her and she let them focus on her former body that was ready for rest, laying in stillness on the bed. She looked down at her new body while she embraced the gratitude of being younger and healthy. "Thank you again, Ella," she said to the quiet room.

Josephine's soul and consciousness, now in Ella's body, walked from the bedroom to the sitting room, where she picked up the hotel phone. The front desk answered within two rings. "Yes, this is Ella Turner in the Legacy Suite. Call an ambulance immediately. Something has happened to Josephine."

Ella sat on the sofa and rung her hands. Tears of relief mixed with shame leaked from her eyes. She jerked a tissue from the box on the table next to her and let the box topple over onto the floor. *Stop this crying, it's all for the best. There's a higher principle at stake. So many people who need help and they are your way home.*

Soon the paramedics were in the bedroom with Josephine's body and Officer Dusky walked into the sitting area. "Ella, are you okay?" He waited for a response. He took a step closer and increased the volume of his voice. "Ella?"

Remembering that was her name now, she sat upright with a start. "Yes, I'm fine." She went with the roll she assigned herself and dabbed the corner of her eyes with the tissue. "It was just so sudden. Josephine was fine, and I went to take in her medication…" She covered her mouth with the back of her hand just as the paramedics wheeled the body that was covered and strapped onto the stretcher past the doorway. She looked away with a loud gasp.

Dusky sat on the edge of the sofa next to her and let the silence take over the moment. "It's okay," he said. "She lived a full life and was ill." He patted her shoulder and stood up. "It will take some time to accept but, given everything, there was nothing anyone could have done." After finding a new place to settle in a chair across from the sofa, he took out his notepad. "Take your time and tell me what happened."

Just when Ella was done recounting an edited version of events, Officer Dusky turned his head in response to a knock on the entryway door to the suite. Without a word, he went and answered.

The young hotel concierge walked in with the police officer. The concierge looked at Ella with sad eyes. "Ms. Turner, we've prepared another room for you. We figured you would be more comfortable there for the night."

"That's very thoughtful." Ella rose from the sofa. "Just give me a few minutes to pack my things."

The concierge nodded. Before walking out with Dusky, he said, "I'll be in the hallway when you're ready."

Alone in the suite, Ella went to her room and opened her suitcase. She packed all her clothes and walked down the hall to the bathroom. After gathering her things into a small tote bag, she turned off the light and went to retrieve her luggage. In the suite's stillness, she could hear her steps on the wooden floor. A shiver ran across her shoulders, and she sensed someone was following her from behind. She spun to look back, and a tiny spike of adrenalin moved through her body. "Hello?" she called out. Her eyes searched down the hallway to see if the concierge had returned to check on her, but there was no one. Turning back in the direction she was headed, she willed her heart to return to a normal pace. *The boy got it right. A different room would be better.*

Chapter Four

After their private anniversary dinner in the conservatory, Darian returned with Grace to their oversized bedroom. There were three vases of red roses that Darian had Henry, the attendant, bring up and arrange around the room. Grace left the flowers unacknowledged and disappeared into the bathroom. Darian filled his glass from the bar and settled on the loveseat. He sat on the side closest to the balcony doors so he could feel the breeze and see part of the night sky. With a stretch of his legs, he put his feet up on the sturdy but embellished coffee table and leaned back further. *What a life. Now I get to make love to my wife.*

He sipped his drink. The bathroom door opened, and he turned to see Grace walk over in a blue, flowing nightgown. Grace didn't even glance at him and, as if by habit, headed to sit in one of the chairs across from the loveseat.

"Oh, come on now. Sit over here." Darian patted the decorative throw pillows next to him.

Grace changed her direction and sat on the other end of the loveseat. After a silence, she said, "It was a lovely dinner. And I can't remember the conservatory looking so vibrant. The new gardener is working out well."

"Yes, everything was great." He set his drink on the end table. "Happy anniversary, dear." He leaned towards Grace. She moved in his direction with a short flinch, followed by a scan of his face. Darian's approach remained slow but steady until Grace met him for a soft touching of their lips. Her lips felt so smooth and almost creamy that passion crept into his stomach. Before the kiss ended, he tilted his head to the side and let the soft kiss turn into deepening kisses. Grace ran her hand up his shoulder and slid it around his back.

Darian figured it was smooth sailing from there and slid his body closer to her until he could place a hand on her thigh. A gusty breeze through the patio doors encompassed them. He was lost in the moment, yet it was like watching a scene in a movie. He slid his hand up her thigh to her waist. Their lips were moving in rhythm, so he glided his hand to the small of her back and, using a slight pressure, he encouraged her to move closer to him. With that, Grace pulled away as she sucked in a quick breath. Not being done yet, she placed a hand on his chest and pushed him back. She stared at him while he thought he'd never seen somebody look so confused.

Darian stayed still and watched Grace smooth out the shoulders and bottom of her nightgown. For a definitive ending, she re-situated to sit facing forward on the loveseat. He could feel himself searching the residue from the previous soul that was in his body while his eyes were searching her every movement for some idea of what was happening. He felt something strong and bold, yet gritty and raw.

Grace turned to look at him in a snap of a second. "So, where do you want it?"

This time, Darian pulled away from her. He felt his mouth twitch, but no words formed.

She stared at him until she let out a sigh. "I guess right here, then?"

Still trying to process the shifting energy in the room, he remained speechless, keeping a watch on her actions. She got up, stood in front of him, and put one hand on his knee. When she used it to steady herself as she knelt to the ground, he sat up straight. Kneeling in between his knees, Grace's face turned stiff, and she unbuckled his belt.

"No, wait." His mind put everything together, and he understood the feeling he had a moment ago. It wasn't pleasure. It was the feeling of taking something away from Grace's inner self. A feeling of harm. He grabbed her hands and pulled her up to a standing position with him. "Really, you don't have to…"

"What do you mean? We both know that's all it's going to be. I'll take care of you, and you'll say you're tired. It's time to go to sleep." Grace shook her wrists to free her hands. "What's with the whole romantic seduction scenario tonight?"

He kept his hands wrapped around her wrists but looked at the floor. He shook his head back and forth. "No, no. Let's not do this." He sat back down and met her eyes. In them, it was there again, a hint of fear. This time it was alongside what could only be intense resentment. It was all out in the open for him to see. He shook his head again with his own disdain for the previous man, who must have spent years degrading this likable woman. "Please, let's just sit close."

Grace looked away for a long couple of seconds before saying, "Fine, let me get a glass of wine." She walked across the room.

"That sounds like a good idea. Wheel the whole damn mini bar over here." Darian waved his hand in the air before picking up his drink for a hearty swig.

Grace wheeled the bar over and filled her glass. She sat down next to him and took a few sips of her wine before setting the glass on the coffee table. Still sounding curt, she asked, "What should we do now?"

"Come here." Darian snuggled her closer to the crook of his arm. "Talk to me like a stranger." He grinned. "Pretend you don't know me and tell what your day is like."

She looked at him with her eyes stretched wide open. Before he could react, her expression relaxed and she laughed. "That will be easy. You don't know what my day is like, anyway."

Chapter Five

Zofia pulled her tan station wagon into the circular drive. Her eyes traveled over the stone walls of the Whitmore mansion up to the roof. She was so distracted she almost clipped the lawn, but she navigated the curve with a quick reaction. Her mind went back to debating if she should take this fluffy job for a bunch of rich people. Some might think they could get closure from death through a psychic medium telling them everything was okay. And if it didn't turn out to be okay, they could blame her and laugh at the eccentric, entertaining phony. It might be a waste of her talents and a waste of her time. "Well, I'll go see what this woman wants," she said out loud as she put the vehicle in park. She got out and walked up the steps. It took her a minute to find the doorbell in between the massive front doors.

One door opened and a young man in an impeccable uniform stood on the other side of the threshold. "Welcome to the Whitmore estate." He took a moment to scan down to her waist without changing his expression. "How can I help you?"

Now self-conscious about her choice of attire, she straightened her flowing, multi-colored blouse. "Hello, I'm Zofia. I have an appointment with Ms. Whitmore."

The house attendant stepped aside and raised his arm, gesturing her to come inside. "Of course. She's been expecting you. Right this way."

Zofia followed the attendant into the large entryway. She felt her eyes widen as she looked around her. The high cathedral ceiling towered over her, and decorative molding framed the space from the floor to the ceiling. Her eyes scanned across from the entrance, where a wide staircase, lined with elegant banisters, lead up to the second floor. The staircase, covered in plush looking maroon carpet, ended at a large landing framed by decorative windows.

She returned her gaze to where she was standing and the area opened up to two large hallways, one on each side. Henry had already gained a few steps on her down one of the hallways, so she hurried her pace. When they turned the corner into the parlor, a woman who was sitting at a table and chairs stood up and smiled. Sun streamed in through the window behind her and outside a glimpse of where the sea meets the land stole the view.

"You must be Zofia. So nice to meet you. I'm Grace," the woman said.

They exchanged introductions before Grace lead Zofia over to the table. "Please make yourself at home. Would you like something to drink? Tea perhaps?"

Zofia took a seat in one of the carved wooden chairs on the other side of the table from where Grace was getting settled. The chair was sturdy but creaked with age as she got comfortable. "Tea would be nice. Something herbal, if it's no trouble."

Grace looked at the attendant, who was still standing with perfect posture just inside the door. "Henry, tea, please. And bring the herbal collection so Zofia can pick something she likes." After that, Grace smoothed her hand across the marble tabletop then extended a downward smile in Zofia's direction. "I asked you here about having your services for a charity event. But I'm afraid it's been delayed." She looked out the window. "We received news early this morning that Josephine, the board member we were working with, passed away." She breathed in and released a long sigh. "She was a good friend."

Zofia allowed a moment to pass. "My condolences. Changes like those are difficult, but be assured spirit will guide the way."

Grace turned back in Zofia's direction. "Thank you. I suppose you're right." She adjusted in her chair. "Well, I still would like to meet with you. After the appropriate time has passed, we plan on going ahead with Ella, the executive director, as the liaison to the charity."

Without calling attention to himself, Henry had returned and was placing everything for tea service on the table. He opened a box for Zofia that contained a large variety of teas, and she chose a packet of peppermint tea, one of her favorites. He served Grace, closed the box, and set it on the table. "Will that be all, ma'am?"

"Yes, thank you, Henry." Grace smiled and nodded before Henry left the room. She bobbed her tea bag in the hot water a few times before her face brightened. "That is such a lovely blouse you're wearing. The bright colors seem to soak in the sunlight and they complement your dark hair."

Zofia looked down at her ruffled shirt and fluffed it so the billows flowed down her robust torso. She leaned closer to Grace and said in a low whisper, "Oh, thank you. I was worried it was a bit much."

Grace leaned back and giggled. "No, I think it's lovely." She picked up her teacup. "So, tell me a little about yourself and what you do." She took a sip of tea while keeping her eyes on Zofia.

"Well, as you know, I'm a spiritualist and a psychic medium. As a medium, I'm able to connect with spirits. All mediums have different methods, but I'm able to see images of spirits and interpret the messages they send to loved ones. Many times, those who are returning to The Origin sense when a loved one needs their presence and will leave a message."

Grace set down her tea. "Oh, it's more involved than I expected. Forgive me, I thought it was just some kind of vibe you pick up on. But you see them?"

Zofia nodded and lifted her teacup with the saucer. She said nothing about the spirit of the young boy sitting on the floor next to Grace. He seemed content while playing with toy wooden blocks that were spread out around him.

"So, what if you miss their message? I mean, if it's left when they are leaving, it seems it's only available for a short time." Grace ran her fingers on the side of her teacup and shrugged.

Zofia finished her sip of tea. "Sure, that's a fantastic question. It's just that in spirit's realm, there is no such thing as time. The message is always in the mailbox, so to speak." She laughed and set the saucer with the cup on the table. "That is, until it's been delivered and, once it is, the spirit finds more peace in The Origin."

"I apologize, but I was looking for entertainment, you know, for a party. I don't think all our guest would be open to such a thing."

"That's understandable." Zofia reviewed her thoughts about this situation again before saying, "That part is up to you. Sometimes mediums extend information to those who aren't open to hearing it while hoping it's still helpful. But your point of view is correct. In that case, it's often interpreted as entertainment." Zofia picked up the saucer and teacup again. Out of the corner of her eye, she noticed the young boy spirit turn to look towards the entryway of the parlor. Then he disappeared.

"What I think we could do is…" Grace's eyes looked past Zofia.

The same as everyone else, Zofia shifted her sight towards the entrance. A man was striding into the room with a grin on his face. She couldn't believe what she was seeing and closed her eyes tight before refocusing. A murky green haze surrounded the man and in that haze were many spirits. She tried to count. There were five, ten, maybe a few more. Her hand holding the saucer with the teacup on it shook. In her mind, it was as if the man was approaching in slow motion. It took restraint for her not to jump out of the chair and run away from this specter.

"There's my lovely wife," he said, as he kept walking closer.

She could see the trail of spirits that surrounded him more clearly now. Some she could barely make out in the murky haze. Those looked sad and depleted, like emaciated beggars on the street. Others could be seen with clarity, including a young man with dark hair. That one stared at her as the group moved even closer. The sight made her gasp and the teacup wobbled, splashing tea onto her hand and the saucer. She used her free hand to steady the tea and set it on the table. After staring downward for a moment, she gathered the courage to look at everything again. Now, more of the vibrant spirits were staring at her with lucidity in their eyes. It was at that moment she knew this differed from the messages she received. These spirits weren't images. They were still intact, still intermingled with consciousness. They were trapped. Trapped in this man's energy field, in a ghoulish prison where they were aware of being in a suspended state.

"Honey, this is Zofia. We we're talking about the charity event." Grace smiled at her husband. "Zofia, this is my husband, Darian."

"Hope you don't mind if I interrupt for a minute," Darian acknowledge Zofia with brief eye contact.

Zofia had shifted in her chair and hung on to one of the wooden arms with all her might. She tried to relax her posture and the look on her face, but all she could do was produce a close-lipped smile. The phenomena surrounding Darian were unearthly and rare.

"What's on your mind?" Grace asked her husband.

Darian drew even closer and, not wanting to get into his tainted aura, Zofia leaned away. He leaned over closer to Grace. Zofia leaned further away from him until one leg of the chair lifted off the ground. It was a leg under the table, so she went with it, and grabbed the edge of the heavy marble top to steady herself while hoping the chair didn't creak in protest.

Darian stayed close to Grace and whispered, "I wanted to make sure we're still having lunch on the balcony today."

"Yes, see you then." Grace leaned back and patted his shoulder.

Darian stood up straight. "Nice to meet you. Zofia, was it? Unusual name."

Zofia managed a half-hearted smile and nodded without saying a word and, in return, Darian met her eyes for a few intense seconds. Then, the same way he strode in, he strode out of the room. Zofia's stiff muscles loosened, and she let all four chair legs rest on the floor, but she never stopped watching the man and the cloud of spirits surrounding him until they were out of sight.

"Are you okay?" Grace asked. "I hope my husband's interruption didn't bother you."

"No, no," Zofia choked. She noticed the spirit of the young boy with his toy blocks return and felt a little lighter.

Grace shook her head before refocusing on her tea. "Something about him has changed."

"Something changed, you say?" Zofia leaned forward and rested her hands on the table in a light grasp. "Like what?"

"It's hard to put into words." Grace gazed towards the door. "It's little things, like just now. That's not something he would have done in the past." She looked in Zofia's direction. "But it's almost like his personality has changed. Almost like—"

"Almost like he's someone else?"

"Yes, I guess so." Grace grinned. "I'm not complaining, though. Things have been pleasant."

"That's nice." Zofia grew a genuine smile.

Grace laughed with a light blush creeping into her cheeks. She composed herself and pulled her chair closer to the table. "Back to the charity event. What I was thinking is that you could attend as our guest. I appreciate what you do, and it would be a pleasure if you could join us. You could get to know everyone, see how they respond to you, and we could go from there."

Zofia liked Grace from the moment they met. In that regard, she looked at the boy spirit with his message waiting to be unlocked and thought that would have to wait for another time. Then she looked back at the door and thought about what had just happened. She didn't understand what she encountered, but despite her desire to run, she wanted to find out more. Aunt Rosalie would know what was going on here. Rosalie was part of the long line of mediums within the same family. Each of them had contributed to a historical library that Rosalie knew backwards and forwards. With her mind still in a misty haze, Zofia said, "Sure, I would love to attend."

Chapter Six

On the train to Dewcall, Ella watched the landscape change from rugged coastline to homes on the outskirts of the city. Memories of being Josephine rambled through her mind in tune with the clatter of the wheels moving along the tracks. She let the thoughts go. It was time to get on the ground as the executive director of SecondHope.

The scattered homes turned into a steady stream of neighborhoods, and she could see the larger buildings that formed the downtown skyline in the distance. Dewcall was unique. Located on both sides of the river border between Kapra and Treaton, it was considered the territory of both countries. In the oldest of stories, citizens on both sides of the river built a bridge so they could share in the prosperity brought by each county. To this day, it's a bustle of visitors from both countries and tourists on their way to the Bracemour Mountains to the north. But, given the recent events, it also brought those who were escaping the conflict between Treaton and their neighbor to the east, Atril.

Ella's anticipation grew as she could see the train station around the bend. Drawing closer, she took in the horde of people on the Kapra side. They were pouring off the trains, leaving empty ones to return to the outskirts of Treaton's capital, Mightwell. It looked more chaotic than she expected, confirming this was the place she was meant to be. At the same time, her dislike for the Atrilians grew. *Who do the Atrilians think they are that it's just fine to put people's lives into upheaval? Boys with toys, that's what I think.*

The train jerked a few times from the pull of the brakes as they approached the covered rail area. She made sure all her belongings were back in her carryall bag before the train came to a stop so she could gather her luggage. Out on the platform, she took the walkway over the tracks and became part of the cluster of travelers and refugees. She looked for the signs directing refugees to SecondHope's tent so they could get a hot meal and the supplies they offered.

The crowd thinned out, and the chatter increased as everyone has some room to breathe. Ella looked around and noticed a group of people full of laughter, another with fussing children, and yet another shedding tears from their eyes. Her own eyes encountered a sign with the SecondHope logo, and she headed for the tent. She found Frank, the program director, observing the activity.

Frank gave her a wave before walking to meet her just inside the entryway. With his tall and wiry frame, he leaned over and picked up her suitcase with ease. "Good to see you."

Ella looked around. "It looks like everything is going well."

"We're doing alright." Frank turned to Ella and put his free hand on her shoulder. "I was sorry to hear about Josephine. We all were." He drew into himself for a moment. "I wish I could have made it to the services."

"Oh, you know, she would have wanted everyone to stay here and keep things moving." Ella laughed and gestured her hand to the crowd sitting in folding chairs while filling their empty stomachs.

Frank let out his own laugh. "She sure would have." He bobbed his head up and down. "She was a determined lady."

Ella grinned. "You have no idea." She paused until the moment was over. "Let's get to it. What's the status? What do we need to address?"

Frank lifted the clipboard in his hand and flipped through a few pages. "Everything here is going well. The biggest issue is our facility only has a few remaining beds."

"Almost full, already? Did you get ahold of The Faith of Silence Church yet? Sometimes they can offer space."

"You know them better. I thought you might want to contact them. We can go over what we have in stock first, in case they have extra supplies."

Ella agreed to the inventory, then checked in with other staff and volunteers while Frank loaded her suitcase into the SecondHope van. It took almost as long to get through the traffic surrounding the train station as it did to finish the drive to SecondHope's primary facility. Ella's heart lightened as they walked in the entrance, but she quickly came to halt. She searched around her memories of being a board member and tried to recall where her office in this life was located. She shifted in one direction, then the other.

"Everything okay?" asked Frank.

"Oh, sure." Ella thought for a moment about how to maneuver the details. "I was just wondering if I wanted anything out of my suitcase."

Frank's eyes drifted down the hallway to the left before he said, "I'll go get it. It's no trouble. We both know you'll end up staying in the apartment upstairs." With a turn, he walked back outside.

Ella wasted no time and followed Frank's glance down the hallway. A memory flickered in her mind as soon as she saw a row of office cubicles next to a large window. It was just a little further down. Her name was outside the door, and she released a breath as she went inside where she scanned the small room for confirmation. The desk was overflowing with files and papers. On the wall behind that were a few photos stuck to a corkboard. They displayed her smiling face on most of them, so she felt at ease and settled into the desk chair.

She scanned the files that were top and center. Many of them had sticky notes from Betty, whom she gathered was the executive assistant. Just as she was digging in to make sense of everything, Frank appeared in the doorway. "If you need anything, your bags are upstairs." He used his thumb to point behind him. "Are you ready to go over the inventory?"

Ella stood up. "Of course. I need to call the church today." She followed Frank and was glad to get to know the building in an inconspicuous way. They went through the need for additional blankets and laundry supplies before reaching the kitchen. The space was empty and quiet, aside from the sounds of dishes being washed in the back. She could imagine the large pots as they bumped into the side of the industrial stainless steel sink. Still making her way with Frank to review the dinnerware and dry goods stock, she glimpsed the man washing dishes. He must have been about five or six years younger than her current body, and the complexion of his tan skin accented his chocolate-brown hair. She watched the muscles in his arms flex as he rinsed a large stockpot and used one hand to flip it onto the dish rack. Sensing someone was around, he turned in Ella's direction and they locked eyes. His eyes were like dark brown pools of peace. A comforting place where Ella would be happy to spend some time.

Frank slowed his steps. "Hey, Bonner. How's it going today?"

The dishwasher hesitated before moving his line of sight away from Ella. "It's good. Just prepping for dinner. Everyone will be back soon." He used his apron to dry his hands.

"We can't thank you enough for volunteering." Frank gestured his clipboard in Ella's direction. "This is Ella Turner, the Executive Director."

Without being sure why, Ella felt exposed, and warmth grew in her cheeks as they exchanged introductions.

Frank looked back to Ella. "Bonner's from Mightwell. He came here with his mother and stepsister."

"And how is it we're so lucky to have you volunteer?" asked Ella.

Bonner put his hands on his hips and leaned back against the sink. "Well, our family decided I would be the one to help my mother and stepsister evacuate. While I'm here, it's the least I can do to give back." He turned and adjusted the pot on the dish rack before looking into her eyes again. "My family back home may face things that are much worse."

The apartment above the SecondHope facility was basic, but comfortable. Ella slept well and, with the kitchen downstairs, she needed little. In the morning, she set off to work on the stack of files that dominated her desk. Time got away from her, and she grabbed a few files she was reviewing before getting lunch. In the kitchen, she expected to see Bonner at the sink washing dishes again, but a different volunteer was hard at work. Easier than admitting the hint of disappointment she felt, she smiled and greeted the alternate dishwasher before getting something to eat.

On her way back to the office, Ella cut through the large refugee common room. She scanned the rows of tables, the community television mounted high on the wall, and the children's play area. Many people were out for the afternoon. On most days, it would stay quiet until just before dinner. With her eyes focused across the room, a familiar voice interrupted her inspection.

"There's Ella. Maybe she'll play a hand," Bonner said.

Ella felt the corner of her lips turn upwards as she walked over to Bonner and a girl who was about twelve-years-old, sitting at a nearby table. "What are you playing? It looks like Uno."

"It sure is. This is my stepsister, Olivia. Come, play a quick hand with us." Bonner nodded towards the seat across from him.

Ella smiled at Olivia, then looked back at the door. "No, I should get to work. I've been away and, with everything going on, I'm kind of swamped."

"Come on, play with us. We need someone new to join our game." Olivia exaggerated a frown.

Ella felt a child-like feeling creep into her chest. She looked at Bonner's smile and he nodded in confirmation.

"Alright. Just one game," Ella said. After placing the files on the table, she sat down.

"Yay!" Olivia bounced in her seat and handed the oversized deck to her brother for shuffling.

Their laughter echoed through the common room. Ella kept getting stuck at the draw pile and found more and more amusement with each unplayable card she picked-up. Bonner slimmed down his hand, but when he only had two cards left, Olivia played a wild-draw-four-card and stole the game. As they were quieting down, Ella noticed Frank walk through the room and remembered where she was. Still smiling, she pushed her seat back from the table. "I must get going." She picked up her folders.

"That was so much fun!" Olivia laughed, then ran her hand down her throat. "But I feel like I have a sore throat starting."

Ella scanned Olivia's face. "Your cheeks are a little flushed. I thought it was from all the laughing."

Bonner stood and rested the palm of his hand on her forehead, then flipped his hand to use the back while feeling her reddened cheeks. "You are warm." He dropped his hand to his side. "Why didn't you tell us you didn't feel good?"

Olivia rested her head in one hand. "It's nothing. It just feels a little scratchy."

"Go lay down. I'll bring you something for your throat in a minute."

"Fine," Olivia said, but shot her older stepbrother a look before getting out of the chair.

"I hope she feels better." Ella patted her hand on Bonner's shoulder. "I'm guessing you know where the thermometers and medications are located."

"Yah, thanks." He let out a short laugh. "I stocked the cabinet last week."

Ella nodded. "Just let me know if you need anything." She turned and walked directly to her office. While sitting down, she read the time on the clock and her mood shifted. *Half the afternoon is gone. Just great. What was I thinking, playing card games in the middle of the day?*

After working from stack-to-stack, she found herself alone in the office area. Outside the door, the lights were dim, and the air was still. She dropped files off in Betty's inbox and headed to the small apartment with sluggish steps. In a habitual way, she got ready for bed and got comfortable under the covers. Her sleep was deep, but on her way to waking she got caught in a vivid dream.

Large intricate shapes were floating around her and she realized she was floating with them, closer to the ground. The shapes were beautiful clear crystals with fractal arms that reflected the surrounding light. She looked at her body and found she was one of the shapes. Before she could marvel too long at her new form, she landed with a soft bounce and saw mountains surrounded by blue sky. A hand reached down, and the shadow of a person said, "Let me help you up."

Without noticing, she had transformed into her human body again. She reached for the hand, then felt herself spring to her feet. The shadow stepped closer, and it was Bonner. "Look around you. This is a spiritual place," he said. But before she could look around, he slid his hand up her lower cheek, letting his fingers spread behind her ear. He leaned in and she met his kiss. When their lips touched, it tickled. From there, they fell into a longer kiss that was electric. The kiss embodied her until she heard knocking.

As she became more awake, the dream faded, but the knocking remained persistent. Then she heard a voice. "Ella, are you awake? There seems to be an emergency."

"What? Who is it?" She called out while bouncing out of bed. She grabbed her robe and headed for the door.

"It's me. The night security guard."

Ella unlocked the bolt and flung the door open. "What is it?"

"There's a man who says his sister is sick. That she needs a doctor."

"What time is it? Won't the nurse be here soon?"

"He says her fever is very high. He insisted I get help immediately."

"Alright. Let's go." She nudged the security guard by the shoulder so she could exit the apartment and close the door. At the bottom of the stairs stood Bonner. He had a hand on one hip with the other on the bottom of the handrail. The moment his eyes hit Ella's, his expression shifted, and he stood up straight. "Crap, I'm so sorry to bother you. I've been checking on Olivia all night." He looked back towards the dormitory before saying, "And this time her temperature was much higher. She's not doing well.

Is there anyone who can drive us to the emergency room?"

Ella finished the stairs and rounded the stairwell in the direction of her office. "We have a doctor on call. I'll page him and see if he can come right away." She made her way to the office, thankful the doctor's information was at hand because she had to settle a simple discrepancy in the books.

Looking through a misty fog, Ella waited for the doctor at the door. It wasn't long before she watched him trod up the front steps just as dawn was trying to peek its way over the horizon.

"My dear, here we are again," he said like an old friend.

"I suppose so." Ella opened the door wider for him and took his overcoat.

The doctor seemed to lead the way to the dormitory until his eyes scanned Bonner standing by the entranceway. "Hello. I'm Dr. Donaldson." He shook Bonner's hand. "Let's have a look at your sister."

"Yes, thank you so much for coming. She rarely gets sick like this." Bonner walked with the doctor as they passed the door into the dormitory.

Ella focused her eyes on the entranceway. Of course, everything would be fine and there was no reason to follow them. Besides, it would cross a boundary. It wasn't her place. She tucked her robe tighter around herself and headed back towards the apartment. As she passed the security desk, she slowed her pace to look at the security guard. "If there's anything else needed tonight, wake me."

"Yes, ma'am." He tipped his hat in her direction.

Upstairs, Ella got a drink of water, threw off her robe, and dove back into bed. In the dimness, she turned off her alarm and thumped it back on the nightstand. She laid on her back with an arm over her eyes. If she didn't hear anything soon, she could rest well that a trip to the hospital wasn't necessary. After dozing off, she woke up with a start and looked at the clock. Almost an hour had passed since she went back to bed. She rolled onto her side and tucked a pillow under her head. Her heavy eyes closed and she returned to a deep sleep, only to find that when she opened her eyes again, sunlight was streaming in between the window blinds. Her sight wandered around the room. *What time is it, for God's sake?*

In a fury, Ella got dressed and went downstairs. The watch had ended, and the security station would sit empty until the next night shift. She turned back toward her office and looked for the executive assistant. Betty came around the corner looking chipper. "Morning, Ella. I heard there was some excitement last night."

"Yes, you could say that. Have you heard anything? How's the girl?"

"Last I knew, she was resting. They got her fever down and the doctor gave her antibiotics. They expect her to start feeling better in the next day or so."

"That's good news." Ella let out a sigh and smiled. She looked away and regained her composure. "I mean, glad that's taken care of. I have work to get back to."

Chapter Seven

Ella kept to herself for the next couple of days. She needed to keep a focus on her mission to give to others. To that end, it was easy enough to avoid the common room, but the kitchen was another situation. She fell into conversations with Bonner on a couple of occasions. But she was keen to keep her distance and not let Bonner's deep brown eyes, smooth voice, or muscular arms make her mind wander. It seemed to work because despite all the activity with the refugees, her desk was becoming manageable. Also, by working in concert with Frank, the meal service at the train station and things at the facility were running with little turbulence.

While perched at her normal spot at the desk, Betty rang into her office to tell her Grace Whitmore was on the line. Ella accepted the call with enthusiasm. SecondHope needed all the funding they could get. She picked up the receiver. "Hello, Grace. So good to hear from you."

Grace's upbeat voice came through the earpiece with clarity. "Glad I could get in touch with you. We wanted to extend an invitation. You're welcome to stay at the estate when you come for the benefit."

"That's very kind, but you're doing enough already. I couldn't impose."

"It's no imposition, really. I've hired extra staff for the weekend and the guest wing has been prepared. We insist. It was Darian's idea."

Ella twisted the cord from the receiver around her finger. "I see. In that case, I would love to stay at the mansion."

"We will be so happy to have you. Of course, bring a guest."

Ella softly laughed. "I imagine it will just be me."

The women discussed other details about the benefit before ending the call. Ella's hand let go of the phone while she was already thinking about what to pack. She would have to return to her condo, but there would be time for that later. She refocused on solving the list of inventory shortages Frank gave her earlier that morning.

After finishing the list, Ella stood, stretched her back, then flexed a kink in her neck. Outside of her office, Betty was nowhere to be found. She wandered down the hall where everything was quiet, so she peeked into the common area. A large group of refugees, staff, and volunteers were gathered around the television mounted on the wall. Someone called out, "Turn up the volume."

The tallest man in the group walked close to the television, reached up and turned the dial until the reporter's voice broadcasted across the room. Crossing her arms, Ella approached the area with her eyes fixed on the screen. The woman reporter at the desk was handing over the broadcast to Warren Reuel in the field.

"Thanks Andrea." Warren, in his usual green anorak jacket, waved his hand towards the buildings that surrounded the shot. "As you can see, we are still here in the Treatonian capital of Mightwell. Word from the perimeter forces is that the Atrilian soldiers have surrounded the city, but they have not engaged the Treatonian troops. They are holding steady on the outskirts." He let his hand rest on his waist. "The situation seems to be a cold standoff and tensions in the capital are extremely high." The camera followed him while he took a few steps, so a barricade and soldiers protecting the capital were in the background.

Andrea took the moment to ask a question. "Have you heard anything about the safe corridor for evacuees?"

Warren placed a hand over his earpiece and nodded. "Yah, the safe corridor." This time he gestured his hand to the west. "Our sources say the corridor is clear from Atrilian interference." He shifted and looked into the camera. "I will also mention there are unverified reports that the Atrilian Chancellor will make a statement soon. Hopefully, that would shed some light on what has become a very complicated situation." Warren tightened his lips before saying, "Back to you, Andrea."

The scene shifted back to the newsroom where Andrea tapped a stack of papers on the desk and set them to the side. "We will bring updates on the situation in Treaton as they arrive. And now for our next report—"

Conversations generated from the group in the common room. "Breaking news? Nothing's changed," one man grumbled.

Frank left the group and stood next to Ella. "There's no telling what the Atrilians are going to do."

"It seems that way." Ella let out a breath. "We'll just have to prepare for the long haul."

"That's a good idea." Frank stood in silence for a moment before walking towards the kitchen.

Ella's dislike for the Atrilian's actions amplified through the thoughts in her mind. She was about to return to her office when Bonner called her name. She waited until he was in talking distance to exchange greetings.

Bonner looked down and put his hands on his hips before meeting her eyes. "I, ahh, am going to the base of Bracemour Mountains for a day trip tomorrow. I know it's last minute, but I was wondering if you would like to go with me?"

Ella felt her cheeks get warm, and she took a tiny step back, but her eyes stayed with his. Aware of her body language, she replied, "I'm just surprised by the invitation."

He nudged his chin in the general direction of the mountains. "There's a short hike with an observation area. It's beautiful."

"I haven't been to the mountains in a long time." Once she met his comforting eyes again, the child-like feeling returned and words fell from her lips. "Sure, I guess I'll go."

"Oh, yah?" Bonner flexed his knees, and Ella smiled. "Great. We can catch a ride with Frank to the station and take the train." He took a few steps away before looking back with a smile.

Halfway back to her office, Ella's child-like feeling turned around. *What was I thinking? I just agreed to spend the day with him. In the mountains. So much for not getting distracted.*

Chapter Eight

Zofia knocked on the door. "Aunt Rosalie. I'm here."

As Rosalie opened the door, her smile expanded. She was a short, thin woman who had long black hair mixed with grey strains. With her body adorned in loose fitting linen cloths, she moved with ease. "Come in, come in." She took a few steps back.

Zofia stepped inside the doorway, and Rosalie held out her arms to pull her into a hug.

Rosalie released the light embrace and looked at Zofia. "I've found something very interesting about the man with spirits caught in a greenish field that surrounds him." She led the way further into the house.

Zofia scanned the living room. It was clean but scattered. Books here, papers there, a lone shoe in the middle of the room. "I see nothing has changed."

"No, not really." Rosalie took a few more steps. "Everything we need is in the library." She opened the door to expose the room that consumed the back half of the house. Each wall was lined with rows of shelves brimming with books from ceiling to floor. Sunlight came in from a few windows and shined upon a large table in the middle of the room. On the end of the table closest to the door was a dish of sandalwood incense next to an ornate incense burner, and on the far end were a few stacks of books.

Rosalie walked over and took an incense cone out of the dish and lit it to start a flame. "A little extra cleansing never hurts," she said. With a puff of air from her mouth, she blew out the fire and the end of the cone turned into a smoking ember. She lifted the top of the incense holder and placed the cone inside. Once the lid was on the holder, smoke floated out of the decorative holes. She leaned close and used her hand to waft the scented smoke towards her chest before getting comfortable in one of the leather seated chairs at the table.

In a ritualistic fashion, Zofia did the same with the incense smoke and sat across from Rosalie. She watched as the older woman opened one of the over-sized books to a page where a bookmark was placed.

"You see, it's here." Rosalie tapped her finger on the page. "I believe you've come across a soul hopper."

Zofia leaned over to get a glimpse of the black and white illustration on the page. It showed two people walking hand in hand with spirits surrounding them in a mist. Some of the spirits were clear and vibrant, while others were hazy and worn. Then she noticed a light glow that surrounded their eyes. "That looks just like what I saw, except for the eyes." She pointed at the illustration. "What is that? It looks like light radiating from them."

"I'm not sure. Maybe it's symbolic of the knowledge of souls that they possess. The text briefly refers to it as the light of life." Rosalie returned her focus to other parts of the passage. "Although the soul hoppers seem unreal, the history is well documented. They are two souls that when they last returned to The Origin, instead of mixing with many souls, their souls immediately intermingled with one another."

She flipped to the next page. Streams of sunlight revealed the incent smoke mixed with dust that swirled in the air.

"Because they only intermingle with one another, soul hoppers always return to earth as a pair, each with knowledge about souls. And when they make the choice inside themselves, they become entranced to push the soul out of another human so they can inhabit the body. Incomplete apart, they are destined to move from body-to-body on earth until they find one another again."

Zofia leaned back in her chair. "Sure, that explains the husband, but there was only him. Grace, the man's wife, didn't have a spirit cloud. And she had a message waiting from a loved one. Everything about her seemed ordinary."

Rosalie gave her direct eye contact and leaned forward. "I assure you there is another. Also, the attraction between the two will be strong. They return with opposite qualities from one another, yet at a deeper level carry the same knowledge." She sat up and scanned the book. "Some say they are intertwined reflections of one another."

"So, what happens when they get together?" Zofia asked.

"When their souls come together through a union of both mind and body, it will be a love so intense that it creates a powerful force. For them, they are released back to The Origin and are blessed by becoming one with all things." Rosalie held up a hand then shifted to moving her finger down the page. "For the soul-spirits caught in their wake, they experience a spontaneous release followed by a deep bliss until they reach The Origin. After that, they continue their journey as it was before."

"It was disturbing to see the spirits were lucid, conscious even." Zofia's gut churned at the thought.

"Um, yes." Rosalie nodded with emphasis before saying, "Then, for the world around the joined soul hoppers, there is a ripple effect. A ripple effect of healing for miles and beyond."

The two women sat in silence for a moment until Zofia adjusted herself in the chair. "What will this ripple effect of healing be?"

Rosalie shrugged. "It doesn't give many specifics. It just says that the power from their joining will radiate, like never-ending ripples, until everyone benefits from the joining of two soul hoppers." She placed her hand on top of Zofia's. "Is there a way you can see the husband in a social situation? One with lots of people he knows around?"

"Why me? What am I going to do?"

"You can see the spirits caught in their wake. If you find the other soul hopper, you can encourage them to get together. Even if the soul hoppers are near one another, they may not discover the other for generations, and the benefit of their rejoining would be delayed."

Zofia looked down and used her finger to trace the grain on the old wooden table. "Fine. I already agreed to attend their charity party. There will be many guests."

Rosalie stood and slapped the book shut. Her voice raised to a high pitch as she said, "Perfect. See if the other soul hopper is there."

Zofia pushed herself away from the table and mumbled, "Wish I had your enthusiasm."

Chapter Nine

Despite her inward battle, Ella met Bonner for the trip to the Bracemour Mountains as planned. Cozy in warm jackets and hiking boots, they took the train north to the park's entrance. Then a smaller tram took them further into the park to the trail leading to the observation point.

"Is there anything else you need? We can make a stop at the general store before we go," Bonner said.

"I'm fine." Ella pulled a crocheted hat out of her coat pocket and put it on her head. "I hope this hike isn't too difficult."

"Oh, no. You'll be fine." Bonner adjusted his pack, then clapped his hands together. "Let's go."

They hiked the rest of the morning through the trail lined with mature evergreen trees before getting sight of the viewing area. Another couple was leaving, and that left a group of three hikers lingering in the small space. Ella and Bonner stepped up to the guardrail with a full view of the mountains that surrounded them. It reminded her how the mountains are so expansive that they fill your chest and why the park touts that they have the highest elevation on the continent. Her eyes scanned the combination of smooth surfaces at the base that contrasted with jagged rock that formed the snow-covered peaks.

"There's something about this place. I don't know…" Bonner scanned across the horizon. "The feeling reminds me of being in Ecrad. The port city."

"I've never been to Ecrad." Ella slid closer to Bonner.

"You haven't? How could you not visit the sacred city? It's incredible."

"Tell me."

"It's hard to put into words." He looked at Ella, while resting against the rail. "It's something about the way it feels." He closed his eyes and sucked in a deep breath through his nose. "This reminds me how the people of Ecrad created a sacred energy stone by drilling into the ground in the middle of the city, then joined that with a tunnel that runs into the sea waters. Then they filled the spaces with the wet stone from the quarry and molded it to reach above the land and into the water." He looked back at the mountains. "Some people who live in town say when things get quiet at night, you can feel the rhythm of the ocean. That the earth's embrace focuses the beat of the water's heart."

Ella drew an enormous smile. "Yes. It makes sense this place reminds you of that. You know about the legend of the Bracemour Mountains, right?"

"Just that a lot of climbers have lost their lives on the way to its peaks."

"The thing is, it's well known by mountain climbers that, past a certain altitude on the mountains, compasses get thrown off. They stop working. There're many stories of explorers and hunters getting lost in the mountain's depths." Ella stalled her words while the other bunch of hikers laughed, then returned to the trail. "The native people say it's the Gods testing those who dare to enter the spiritual realms in the mountains." She pulled one shoulder up. "The scientists say it's probably iron deposits deep in the rock that effect the compasses."

"It seems the mountain has a heartbeat of its own." Bonner smiled.

Finding themselves alone in the observation area, they shifted to the middle of the platform and gazed at the horizon. An icy grey cloud was floating into their line of vision. The wind caught the cloud's burst of fluffy snowflakes, so they sailed into the light of the sun.

Bonner pulled Ella's shoulder, so they were facing one another. "There's nothing like watching snowflakes float to the ground." He looked to the sky until the small snow cloud revealed part of the sun. "Some snowflakes land on the cold mountain tops and last a long time." He joined eyes with Ella. "Others land on a warm surface and last only a moment." He wiped a melted snowflake away from her cheek. While leaning closer, he said, "I don't care which, just as long as a snowflake is allowed to be a snowflake."

His lips almost brushing hers, Ella hesitated. This wasn't what she had planned. This was way beyond a distraction. Bonner inched forward and left no distance between their lips. The kiss was soft and lingering. It was enough to shift the tone, and the moment they parted she didn't want it to end. She ran her hands up his arms and embraced him. He responded likewise and brought his lips back to hers, all the time pulling her closer. The prolonged kiss ended when sunlight returned in full force. Still in an embrace, they looked around to see an illuminated snow-filled sky.

After a couple of heartbeats, Ella pulled back and let her eyes examine Bonner's face while her fingers traced his temples and hairline. She let her lips gravitate to his again. This time in their kiss, she left her thoughts by being in the moment, left her sight by submitting her closed eyes to the darkness, and left her other physical senses by letting the intoxication run through her body.

Back in the entrance area, Ella's trajectory for the tram was side-stepped when Bonner grabbed her hand and spun her, so she looked in his direction. "Let's have dinner at the inn. It's a stop along the way to the train station."

His enthusiasm made her smile, but she felt edgy inside. "I really need to get back."

"Come on. There's plenty of time." He smiled and glided his lips in for a quick kiss.

She hesitated, but the child-like feeling had turned into an adult feeling of lightness. "I guess we have to eat. Right?"

Still holding her hand, Bonner flexed his knees. "Right. Next stop, Bracemour Inn."

They walked hand-in-hand and got into line for the tram. After a cozy ride on the overfilled vehicle, they arrived just outside the inn. The building was much larger and, despite its rustic exterior, a bit more modern than she expected. But, as expected, it was set in the heart of the woods and when she let her eyes follow the smell of a campfire, she noticed a large chimney on the roof spewing out smoke. *This isn't romantic at all. What have you gotten yourself into now?*

Inside, Bonner talked with the hostess and soon they were led past a large, round fireplace to a table by the windows. A few flurries glided in and out of view while the sunset changed the color of the sky. They reminisced about the hike while sharing an appetizer. And it wasn't long before the server brought their main courses, steaming hot, from the kitchen.

Ella ate a bite of mashed potatoes and relished their smooth texture. The tastes of decadent ingredients intermingled with the creamy potatoes brought her mouth alive.

"They are good, aren't they?" Bonner used a fork to raise a bite of potatoes from his plate to his mouth.

Ella looked at his eyes, and she could almost see a twinkle. He seemed to delight in simple pleasures in a way that made them innocent. As if they were without cost or reward. They just were. "You're a special person," she said.

"As are you Ms. Ella Turner." He leaned over the table to get closer so he could whisper, "It makes me wonder if we should get a room at the inn tonight."

It took all of Ella's energy to keep her expression stable while maintaining his eye contact. She held on until he leaned back and slid his napkin across his mouth. "I don't know about you, but today was even better than I expected, and tomorrow is Saturday. It's perfect timing for a special night between us." He slid his hand across the table and stroked her fingers.

Ella sat up in her chair and looked at his hand, leaving hers at rest. The slide of his fingers stirred the lightness in her chest. Her mind silent, she felt everything was happening in slow motion. She blinked more than once to bring herself back to real time and looked out the window. The sun had almost set, and dark orange colors streaked across the horizon. That's when she wondered if his kiss would make everything all right and looked back into his eyes.

As if Bonner heard her thoughts, he set down his napkin and rose with a slow intensity. He stepped around the table to get closer to her and placed a hand under her chin. He looked into her eyes. The peace that she saw in them the day they met returned with an overwhelming presence. Their lips touched for a moment and no words passed, but they both knew they were staying in the mountain's heartbeat for the night.

Just before Ella's eyes opened, she wondered where the masses of chirping birds came from then she remembered she was in the suite at the inn. Bonner was lying on his side facing opposite of her, his rhythmic breathing told her he was still asleep. She put her arm across her eyes. *Now you've done it. He's gonna be hard to shake. Although…*

Ella grew a grin and pulled the sheet up to her chin. The memories of last night came into focus. In all the lives she experienced, being with Bonner was the most pleasure she could remember. The way it felt was erotic yet seemed so pure. It reminded her of her last transfer when she went into Ella's body. A pleasure that ran deep inside of her until it seemed to burst out of the top of her head. She watched Bonner stir and rubbed her hand across his warm shoulder. His breathing leveled, and he moved in her direction. She shoved the memories back into her mind. There was just enough time to jump out of bed and grab her coat to use as a robe.

"Hey, wait." Bonner reached out a hand. "What's the rush?" He shifted and sat up on his elbows.

A new feeling took over Ella as she tried to gather her clothes that were strewn across the room. She was still missing a sock when she headed for the bathroom. "You know, it's Saturday. The train doesn't run as often." Hanging onto the door, she looked back at Bonner. "Everything has been wonderful." Unable to hold back a smile, she waited until she could keep a normal expression to say, "But we should get a move on." She closed the door.

In the bathroom, Ella got dressed and made herself look presentable. When she opened the door, Bonner was sitting on the side of the bed, about to put his shirt on. He let go of the shirt and stood. "Were you looking for this?" He grinned, holding her sock in the air.

"Give me that." She swiped at the sock, but Bonner raised it out of her reach and stepped closer. He wrapped his arms around her and pulled her into his embrace. Ella's eyes returned to his before they shared a lingering kiss.

"There, was that so difficult? I just wanted to get a kiss before you got out of bed."

She whispered into his ear, "I guess not."

Bonner let his embrace slide down her back and leaned back, meeting his eyes with Ella. "Last night was special. That wasn't the kind of connection you can find every day."

Ella tilted her head to the side and nodded.

Bonner let his hands fall to his sides. "But you want to get back to SecondHope."

She tilted her head to the other side. "Well, yes." She took a small step back. "The longer the standoff goes on, the more I dislike the Atrilians."

"I didn't know you felt like that."

"Sure, sometimes. Don't you?"

Bonner stepped away and grabbed his shirt off the bed. He pulled it over his head before saying, "It won't do any good to blame the Atrilians. Countries have arguments all the time. Just like people. And those two countries have a long history."

Ella took in his face, and something inside of her rumbled. She liked the way Bonner looked at the world. He seemed to have a smoothness she didn't. "You have a point. Besides, I've dedicated my life to SecondHope. To giving to others, no matter the sacrifice."

Bonner grabbed his hiking boots and moved to one of the chairs next to a small table. While leaning over to put the boots on, he looked at Ella. "Just as long as it doesn't get you into trouble."

Ella took the other chair and gave him a hard glance while putting on her boots alongside him. "How would I ever get into trouble? That's silly."

Chapter Ten

In the bedroom at the Whitmore mansion, Darian settled into what has become his normal spot on the loveseat next to the balcony. He sipped his night cap and let himself sink into the comfort of the surroundings.

It wasn't long before Grace came into the room. "You're settling in a little early tonight." She put down her handbag and sat on the loveseat.

"It's not that early." He chuckled and took another drink. "I have a meeting with Baker & Ganovich tomorrow morning."

Grace placed her elbow up on the back of the loveseat and looked at Darian. "If things hadn't been so different lately, I wouldn't bring this up, but can I ask you about something?"

Darian set his drink down and shifted in her direction. "Of course."

"Promise you'll be open-minded?"

He put his hand in the oath position and nodded his head.

"Remember the medium I interviewed?" She looked away for a moment. "I was straightening the chairs in the parlor after we met, and I found this." Pulling her hand out the side pocket of her pants, she displayed a toy block. A small, rectangular, red block.

"Don't let that stuff get to your head," he snorted. "It's just a toy building block. What's the big deal?"

Her response came quick and strong. "How can you ask me that?" She shook the block, bringing it closer to his face. "You know exactly what it's about."

Darian turned his head away and looked out over the balcony. *I have no idea what this is about. Think fast.*

He grabbed her wrist and tore the block from her fingers. "This is upsetting you so much. Give it to me. Just forget about it."

"Just forget about it?" She stood and placed a hand over her heart. "Just forget about our son? Blocks were Jonathan's favorite toys. For goodness' sake, he took them everywhere." Her face scrunching up, she reached for the toy block, and he let it go into her grasp.

Trying to smooth things over, he put out his arms. "I'm sorry. Here, come sit with me."

Grace put her free hand on her forehead and fell onto the loveseat, facing Darian. He put an arm around her to rub the back of her shoulder. With that, she lowered her head and cried. She let out a few quick sobs, then drew in her breath. Without looking up, she said, "It was all my fault. He was just a boy, and I should've driven him to preschool that day. I didn't. I supervise the estate staff, and I should've noticed the driver had taken to drinking. I didn't." She lifted her head and looked him in the eye. "You know it's true, because that's when you stopped wanting me."

"No, no, no. It wasn't your fault." He kept rubbing her shoulder until she let go of her relentless stare and lowered her head again. A silence passed through the room, so the sound of the waves on the sea took over for a brief second. He thought, *You'll have to wing it. Say something more.*

"I never stopped wanting you. That had to do with me." He nuzzled his head closer to hers. "I felt responsible too. I wasn't even around. I wasn't a good father."

Grace lifted her head and looked at him. "What has made you change?"

"I mentioned it but, I tell you, when I saw that caterer fall to the floor, it stayed with me." He looked across the room for a moment. "It made me think about what I was missing out on." He sat up straighter. "I realized that the best way to honor Jonathan was to be a better man. To be a better husband." He rubbed Grace's shoulder again and pulled her just close enough so he could rest his chin on her shoulder.

She leaned back and scanned her eyes across his face. Her look softened, and she traced her fingers up his jawline. Then she adjusted and moved her lips closer to his.

Darian let her get a little closer before responding likewise. When their lips came together, the pleasure roused inside of his body was more intense than he expected. Yet, for the first time in all his lives, he didn't care that the brief pleasure would be the highlight of the night.

As scheduled, Darian walked into the offices of Baker & Ganovich and didn't have to say a word. The well dressed, attractive receptionist stood and gave him a bright smile. "Right this way, Mr. Whitmore." The receptionist led him past the extravagant office sign. It boasted the law firm as having the most experience with international trade in the country.

She looked at him before opening the conference room door. "Of course, you'll be meeting with Gene and Wilma."

The conference room was small, but its decor felt like a comfortable room at home. Sunlight streamed through the window that was lined with heavy red drapes. In front of the window was a table flanked by two large leather chairs. On the table was a coffee urn, juice carafes, and a tray of breakfast pastries. The rosewood conference table sat in the middle of the room surrounded by four ergonomic looking executive chairs. Darian took one step past the doorway, and the carpet was plush. The man and woman stood and welcomed him as the receptionist closed the door without a sound.

"Please, help yourself," the woman he assumed to be Wilma Ganovich motioned towards the table.

"I'm fine." Darian unbuttoned his tailored suit jacket. "Let's get started."

"In that case, have a seat." Gene Baker slid closer to the table as Darian got comfortable. "As you know, the conflict between Treaton and Atril continues. And the outcome of the standoff could have a significant impact on the profits of your company."

"What are you getting at?" Darian moved his eyes over each of the lawyers' faces.

"Well, as most of the company's imports come from Atril, there's a lot to gain if they would be successful," Gene said.

"It would also be to our benefit if that success would come as quick as possible." Wilma pushed her tortoise-shell glasses up her nose. "Any disruption to production or the ground shipping routes could hurt profits as well as stockholder confidence."

"Of course." Darian adjusted his jacket and leaned to the side. "We have people to anticipate all that. What do you want with me?"

Wilma produced a formal smile. "Sure. We also keep up on predictions about how the war might proceed. You know, predictions from historians and political strategists." She pulled her hands together so they rested on the table in Darian's direction. "You see, they still think the Atrilian's primary interest is in the port city of Ecrad."

Gene nodded. "In addition, we all know if the Atrilians were to gain the port city, the reduction in shipping costs would be lucrative for us, to say the least."

Wilma opened the file folder that was next to her and pulled out a document. "We have identified a non-profit that operates out of Ecrad. They are very sympathetic to the Atrilian's claim to the land." She slid the document in front of Darian.

"We were thinking a sizable donation would help support their preparations in case the control of the city became a source of conflict," said Gene.

Darian scanned the main points on the paper. "Messengers of the New Jurisha? That's a religious affiliation. Their interests are in the sacred sites in the city."

"We're all on the same side. That's what matters," Wilma said. "The donation would be anonymous, of course. Our firm would serve as an intermediary."

Gene removed the cover from a silver pen and handed it to Darian. "We just need you to sign and the money will be transferred."

Protect the company. Reduction in shipping cost. I like that. Darian took the pen in hand and made a dot on the paper. But his thinking altered before he could finish the first stroke. He imagined an untrained group of idealists able to buy whatever military equipment and weapons they wanted. "Wait one minute. Are you saying that you want me to make a six-figure donation to a group of religious rebels to help sway the outcome of the war?" He flicked the pen back down on the table next to the speechless lawyers. "Seems to me putting that kind of money into the wrong hands would cause more conflict." He stood and in three long steps was outside the room.

Darian returned to the mansion and, once inside his bedroom, he threw off his suit in exchange for a blue polo and tan classic fit shorts. He walked out onto the balcony and looked at the sea. The events at Baker & Ganovich churned in his mind. Then, the thought that having an exorbitant amount of money required caution seemed to end any debate. He was fine with his decision whatever happens and ready to get back to enjoying the best of his most recent lifestyle. With the sound of the surf filling the air, he didn't hear Grace approach him from behind. He jerked his head to the side when her hands slid around his waist.

"Would you like to have lunch out here with me?" Grace asked.

"Lunch out here with you would be very nice." Darian slid his hand over her fingers.

Henry was there in no time at all and laid out the balcony table with a bowl of fresh lettuce-salad and a tray of gourmet sandwiches.

Grace used tongs to lift salad onto her plate. "You know, I've been meaning to ask you. The charity event is running a little over budget. Would you allocate more funding?"

Darian chose a couple of sandwiches from the tray. "Why are you asking about settling funds to run the estate again? Can't you take care of all that?"

Grace stared at him. "What do you mean? You've never let me take care of the budget."

He wiped his hands with his linen napkin and tossed it on the table. "That ends now. You know more about how things operate around here than anybody." He stood up and walked into the bedroom. Pushing the intercom talk button, he almost yelled into the speaker, "Get me Tildy, now."

"Yes, of course, sir," said a male voice.

Darian sat on the edge of the bed and bopped his knee up and down until he heard Tildy's voice. "Hello Mr. Whitmore, how can I help you?"

"Set up a meeting with the estate accountants, Grace, and myself. Tell them Grace is taking over the books." He paused before escalating his tone again. "The sooner it gets scheduled, the better."

"I will take care of it right away," said Tildy.

He returned to his chair at the balcony table and eyed his lunch. "Tildy will schedule a meeting. I'll be there for the handoff and will help as long as you need because those accountants, they're so traditional that if they were a book, they'd be leather-bound."

Grace giggled, then raised her hand to her mouth before saying, "You don't know how much this means to me." Her eyes watered.

"What? What is it?" He put down his half-eaten sandwich.

She let out a short laugh before meeting his eyes. "I was so worried. I didn't know what I was going to do if something were to happen to you. How would I run the estate alone? How would I stand strong?"

Darian put up his hand. "That's enough, really."

Grace ignored him and flicked her head to the side. "Not everyone would be nice to a billionaire widow who doesn't have a clue."

He changed his hand gesture and pointed at Grace. "Now, you listen to me." He let his hand down but leaned over the table to give her closer eye contact. "You're an intelligent, capable woman. And you have a strength I've never seen before." Still processing the words he just spoke, Darian leaned back in his chair. "You'll take over the budget because you'll be great at it. Then, if there's anything else we need to cover, we will."

The sound of breaking waves grew louder, and a breeze glided across the balcony. Grace got up and slid into Darian's lap. She put her arms around his shoulders and scanned his face. With a move closer, she kissed his lips. A warm peck at first, but she returned for more intense kisses. Darian glided his hands around her sides and smoothed them up her back.

With their kisses in tune, the passion rose with such intensity it made Darian's stomach buckle, and it reminded him of when he entered his current body.

It was a feeling that could run right through him, if he let it. He moved his mouth to her neck and kissed downwards. Grace let her head relax to the side, and he continued kissing all the way to the base of her throat.

He pulled back and brushed his fingers through her hair. "I feel like we are getting close to the point of no return."

Grace stood from his lap. "God, I hope so." She extended a hand in his direction. Darian stood and placed his hand in hers. Together, they walked into the bedroom.

Once they passed through the doorway, Darian stood enchanted while Grace faced him and unbuttoned the front of her shirt. She turned and walked closer to the bed until she stopped to look over her shoulder while the shirt fell to the floor. He approached her and ran his hand up the length of her arm while taking in the sensation of her soft skin. When their lips met again, they found their way under the covers for the rest of the afternoon.

Chapter Eleven

Zofia pulled her station wagon into the drive at the Whitmore mansion. This time, a porter in full uniform was standing curb-side to meet her arrival. The astute porter collected her bags before leading her through the front door, where Grace was walking across the large entrance hall.

Graced leaned in the porter's direction and told him where to take the bags before addressing Zofia. "We're so delighted that you're here for the charity event and agreed to stay at the mansion for a couple of nights." She clasped her hands and smiled. "I'll take you to your room and you can get settled."

"Your invitation was very generous." Zofia returned the smile.

Grace showed her the way up the steps and down the hall until she stopped and opened a door. "Here we are, a small living area."

"Sure." Zofia eyed the arched ceiling and large window that faced the water. In front of the window was an elegant table and chairs. Then, she turned partway to see her luggage already sitting next to a plush blue couch that accented the tan colored carpet and elegant cream fixtures.

Grace looked around the room. "I imagined you'd be comfortable here." She opened a pair of double doors on one side of the room. "Here's the bedroom, with an adjoining bath."

Zofia eyed the bedroom with a built in four-poster bed. The bathroom door stood ajar to reveal part of a walk-in shower and separate bathtub. She cleared her throat. "More than comfortable. Thank you." With perfect timing, the boy spirit playing with toy blocks had appeared. "Grace, would you like to stay for a moment? It seems you have a message from a loved one."

Grace's expression shifted to a wide-eyed stare, and she tightly crossed her arms.

Zofia knew the look all too well and walked over to the table with smooth nonchalance. She used one hand to pull a chair out from the table. "It wouldn't take long. But it's completely up to you, of course."

Grace looked back at the door before letting her hands fall to her sides. "Sure, why not?" She walked over and sat in the chair across from Zofia. "So, what is it you would like to tell me?"

Zofia sat down in a gentle manner and brought her hands together. "With your permission, I will open the message and do my best to interpret the contents. What the information means may require some input from you."

Grace nodded and got more comfortable in her seat.

"I see a young boy who likes to sit by you while he's playing with toy blocks."

Those were the only words, and Grace's eyes brimmed with tears.

The reaction wasn't unusual so Zofia kept moving forward, using a soft tone as she spoke. "I will sit quietly for a few seconds while I ask to receive the message." She closed her eyes. After the moment passed, she opened them again and took a cleansing breath. "He's showing me the sign for a collision.

Things crashing together." Using her hands, Zofia illustrated by tapping the fingers of one hand into the palm of the other.

Grace got up and retrieved a few tissues from the bathroom and sat back down. "Yes, my son died in a car accident when he was very young."

"But there was blaming. I see a pointing finger. Was there someone held responsible?"

"Yes." Grace ran the tissue beneath her eyes. "They charged our driver with driving while intoxicated, but there wasn't enough evidence to charge him for more serious crimes."

Zofia slid her hand partway across the table. "I'm sorry. I'm sure that was difficult." Then she sat back in her chair. "But I'm seeing the picture for collision again, and it was something else crashing into them." She took another pause before saying, "Yes, I see a green light. The stop light was green. Something crashed into them. Even if your driver was drinking, it doesn't seem it was his fault."

"Oh." Grace's tears increased. "I had thought it was my fault for not driving him myself." She took a deep breath and looked at the ceiling.

"It wasn't your fault. If you were the driver, you could have been harmed too. I understand now why he wanted you to know that." Zofia rested her head to the side and closed her eyes. "I also see the sign for bliss. He's conveying that he didn't suffer and found bliss while in The Origin." Zofia lifted her head and smiled. "And know that he loves you and doesn't want you to be sad."

"I love him, too." Grace let out a burst of tears.

"How do you feel?" Zofia asked.

"Different." Grace let out emotion through multiple small nods. "Lighter, I guess."

"I'm glad. I've been wanting to do that since the last time we met." Zofia's smile grew.

"About the day we met, after you left, I found…" She waved her tissue in the air. "Never mind, I already know." The room filled with silence until Grace looked at Zofia and said, "I hope you'll be joining us for dinner in the conservatory tonight."

"Dinner, in the conservatory…" Zofia looked around, still absorbing her surroundings for a moment. "Sure, I would love to join you."

"Wonderful. Ella Turner, the executive director from SecondHope and her guest, will also be attending."

Zofia stood up from the table. "I look forward to meeting them."

Turning the corner into the lush conservatory, Zofia eyed the stone waterfall sculpture at the far end of the room. The sound of trickling water and moisture in the air enhanced the smell of earth and foliage. She looked upwards to examine the glass ceiling as it let in the changing colors of the sky. With awe, she wondered how anyone could imagine such a lovely room. Grace was moving around a round dining table, eyeing each setting until she looked up and met Zofia's gaze with a smile. The women greeted one another, and Grace was telling her about the plant life in the room when her husband walked in at a quick pace.

"You remember my husband, Darian."

"Oh, absolutely. Nice to see you." Zofia did a slight bow while looking at the spirits around him. Everything seemed the same as last time. Caught in the greenish haze, some spirits looked at her and, accepting their conscious state, she noticed sadness in their expressions. Part of her wished there was something she could do to help, while another part of her still wanted to run away. Run far away from this bizarre ghost story taking place in a cold stone mansion. Just then, another couple entered the room. Zofia stepped backwards with a stumble that almost made her lose her balance. She stared as the woman approached. The woman was just like Darian. There were many spirits caught in a greenish aura that surrounded her. It was the other soul hopper.

"Zofia, this is Ella Turner, whom I told you about." Grace introduced the two women and they exchanged greetings. Next to be introduced was Ella's companion, Bonner.

"Now that we all know each other, let's have a seat." Grace motioned towards the table.

As soon as Ella and Darian took a step towards the table, the spirits in each of their auras noticed the other group and they all clamored to get closer to one another. Some even reached out in an attempt to cross through the energy fields, their hands and arms elongating from the effort. Ella grabbed the back of a chair and slid it partway out. When Darian brushed by her to take a seat on the other side of the table, the spirits shifted, and those surrounding Ella kept moving to stay close to the spirts surrounding Darian. It was like watching a herd of antelope shifting and twisting together as they ran across a landscape. As if pulled by a magnet, Ella let go of the chair back and moved over to sit in the seat next to Darian.

Grace sat on the other side of Darian and, after pushing in the chair for Ella, Bonner took the open seat next to his companion.

With a deep breath, Zofia settled into the last open chair and put her napkin on her lap while collecting her thoughts. Everything was just as Aunt Rosalie described. *I have to do this now. I have to help the soul hoppers get together so there's a chance the spirits can be freed.*

Darian stood and held his glass in the air. "Grace and I welcome everyone to our home. Enjoy the mansion, and explore the grounds. I know I'll spend tomorrow at the pool." He chuckled and placed a hand on his chest. "And I'm sure my lovely wife has one hell of a party in store for us tomorrow. Cheers!" He raised his glass even higher.

Zofia picked up her flute of champagne in tune with the rest of the table and held it up while saying, "Cheers!" She took a sip and licked the fruity taste from her lips.

Henry was already serving salads while everyone got to know each other better. Zofia grazed on her plate while they went through the normal questions people ask about psychic mediums. All the while, she kept an eye on the trapped spirits. She was glad they were focused on each other and somehow pulling the soul hoppers together instead of looking her in the eye.

In due time, the conversation at the table shifted, and Bonner told his story about being a refugee from Treaton with his mother and stepsister. He turned to the side and grasped Ella's hand that was resting on the table. "And that is also how we met."

"That's lovely." Grace set down her fork to put a hand over her heart.

Zofia returned to her champagne as Henry cleared the salad plates in exchange for the main course. He softly said, "Baby lobster with linguini in white sauce," to each person as he set down the warm plate. She twirled a partial strand of pasta around her fork and speared a piece of lobster. Before putting the bite into her mouth, she noticed a break in the conversation. "This mansion must have so much fascinating history," she said.

"Oh my, yes," replied Grace. "Much of the furniture, fixtures, and artwork date back to the beginning of the mansion." She took a bite of lobster with thought in her eyes, then let the fork dangle from her fingers. "Can I tell them about the attic?" She looked at Darian.

Darian returned Grace's eye contact and paused for a moment before saying, "Sure, tell them all about it."

Grace wriggled in her seat. "The mansion was built well over one hundred years ago, and the first owner was an art collector. He wanted a place to hide his treasures, so he put them in the expansive attic." She looked around the table. "As the story goes, since that time, every family has contributed artwork to the vault in the attic."

"How fascinating," Bonner said.

"Yes, and just before the Whitmores took it over, the previous owner made revisions so the attic is climate controlled to preserve the artwork." She looked around the room, then back at the guests. "Wouldn't it be great to do something with all that artwork? To share it with the world?" With a twirl of her fork, she brought a bite of linguini to her mouth and chewed with a smile.

Ella let out a tiny gasp and looked at Grace. "This goes way back, but I'm an art aficionado. What kinds of artwork is up there?"

"That's part of the mystery. Since no one kept an inventory, we're not sure what's been gathered." Grace's thoughtful look returned. "Maybe you could go take a look." She gestured her fork in her husband's direction. "Darian can take you for a tour. It would be wonderful to hear what you think."

"What a rare thing," Zofia said. "It sounds like a great idea they investigate. I'm sure Bonner won't mind if you stole Ella away from him for a few hours." She moved her eyes from Bonner to Ella and then to Darian. She noticed Ella glance at Darian and, when their eyes met, they both were quick to dart their gaze elsewhere.

"Not at all. It seems too interesting to let pass by, and I still need to unpack before bed," Bonner said.

"It's settled then. Darian will take Ella on a tour of the attic after dinner." Grace's smile was even larger than usual.

Soon, Henry cleared dinner plates and served dessert. After fawning over the freshness of the layered sorbet, the conversation faded. Zofia was the first to excuse herself, saying that her day had been incredibly long. Outside of the doorway, she released a sigh of relief even though she knew this was just the beginning.

Chapter Twelve

"The lighting is hardly enough. Take this, and I'll be right behind you." Darian handed Ella a lantern flashlight.

"We have to go up those stairs to get to the attic?" Ella shined the light up the narrow dusty stairwell.

"Yep." Darian wondered how Ella came to have the greenish glow around her eyes just like the old woman. When he looked into them, it felt like they could pull his inner being right into hers. Yet he was so drawn to her, at times all he thought about was her touch. *It's all too strange. I'd rather be sitting on my loveseat in the bedroom, sipping a nightcap.*

They made their way up the stairs, each creaking louder than the last. At the top, Darian caught up with Ella. He had to reach around her to work the pin-pad next to the small door. "Shine the light over here, would you?" he asked.

Ella directed the light, and Darian punched in a short code. The pad beeped, and he was all too aware of how his body rubbed against Ella's as he opened the door. "I've been up here a couple of times. Sometimes I like to roam around the mansion, see what I can find."

They stepped past the threshold, and the smell of the stale stairwell disappeared in the dark climate-controlled room. With Ella a few steps ahead of him, Darian found the industrial light switch and turned on the overhead lighting. The attic spanned the length of the mansion, but with walls added on each side it was a narrow space compared to the foundation of the building. Layered in stands just like oversized magazine racks, countless pieces of artwork settled under dark protective fabric lined each side of the long room.

He looked over at Ella. "Over the top, isn't it?"

Ella looked at him with a hand over her mouth. The other hand still held the flashlight, with its beam shining on the floor. She leaned over and laughed. "This is outrageous!"

"Come on." Darian started walking down the aisle that ran in the middle of the artwork. "There's a few down this way that are easy to get a good look at."

He stopped and bent over. "Here, this one." It wasn't a very large piece, maybe three feet high and a couple of feet wide. He waited for Ella to stand next to him before lifting the cover.

"Oh. Oh." She bent closer and examined the realistic landscape painting of vast mountains. "Lovely oil on canvas. And, if it's authentic, it's a Horace Le Compte. He's an artist who lived in the Bracemour Mountains." She stood up, never letting her eyes off the painting. "That would date it back about a century."

"Here, this way," Darian said.

Keeping her eyes on the painting, Ella turned and stumbled. Darian reached out and grabbed her arm. He took a step closer and pulled her next to him so she wouldn't completely lose her balance. With his hand on her bare elbow, he felt the warmth of her skin and a tingle ran up his forearm. He moved his hand up to her shoulder, but he caught himself from letting it wander up the side of her neck. As Darian stepped back, Ella met his gaze for a brief second.

"Thank you," she said.

"Sure, be careful." Darian pulled his hands and eyes away from her, and in the thick silence that arrived, he looked around the room. He moved ahead and stopped to pull up another cover. "It's one of the smaller pieces, but I like this one."

Ella leaned in and took in the black-and-white picture. "It's a photograph." She put her hand across her chin and got closer. "I don't believe it, but it looks like it's from the Omniscient Mirror Series by Dora Chiasson." She pointed at the print. "See how the light passes through all the glass orbs? Then when your eye travels up the picture, their reflection in the mirror pulls you in?" She shook her head. "There are a few museums who collect this series. You have great taste."

Darian nodded. "Thanks." He felt his face get warm. With a quick turn, he walked further into the attic. *Did I just blush? Get ahold of yourself already.*

Ella kept following his lead and pointed to a piece a few steps away. "That one is huge. It must span eight feet. And what? About five feet high?"

"Yah, that's one I wanted you to see. You'll have to help me with the cover." He got into place on one end of the artwork. "I think it's pretty old, so let's do this careful-like."

Ella leaned down and grabbed the cover at the other end of the artwork.

Darian met her eyes and, in tune, they pulled the fabric outward before lifting it up and letting it fall behind the artwork. He remained quiet while he watched her examine the picture, first from afar, followed by close up. Then she eyed all the way around the edges. For a second, she reached out to touch a corner, but pulled her hand back.

"I'm not sure." She mumbled to herself and scanned the drawing again. "Old is not the word. It's fabric and could date back eight hundred, maybe a thousand years." After giving Darian a side glance, she said, "What else makes it striking is I'm pretty sure it's Atrilian. I haven't seen much Atrilian art, and most of it was in books." She shrugged. "But the colors, the shape of the people, they all fit. And see, Bonner told me about this. In the scene, they're working on the sacred energy stone. It's the connection they made between the land and the sea." She walked up to the drawing and used her finger to point. "It seems to depict them filling the tunnel with wet stone that is gathered from the quarry over here. Then, in the background, they're working on buildings." She let her hand fall to her side. "It's the sacred city of Ecrad."

"That old?" Darian crossed his arms. "Well, what do you know? It supports the Atrilian claim to the land."

"I suppose so." Ella stood close by his side. "How did this ever get here?"

"The first owner of the mansion, the art collector, came from Treaton. He must have been able to get his hands on it."

"If it was stolen during one of the many wars between Treaton and Atril, maybe it should be returned to the Atrilians."

Darian stepped closer to the drawing. *That's a way better move than giving a splinter group a sizable donation for military supplies.*

The silence lingered until Ella said, "Anyway, I'm not certain. You should have an expert look at it."

"Sure. I'd have to figure out the best way to go about everything first. Better to have a plan, in case it's authentic." Still looking at the painting, he tipped his head to the side. "But I think Grace is going to be thrilled."

Chapter Thirteen

After her presentation about SecondHope at the charity event, Ella lifted her gown to walk down the few steps off the stage. With the applause still fading, she took her place in a receiving line a few paces away to connect with guests. The mansion's terrace had been transformed into a magical oasis on a warm night. Closest to the seashore, the extravagant stage was set under a framework of an oversized gazebo wound with small lights that looked like jewels dripping to the ground. She stood on the edge of a small dance floor that was between two clusters of round dining tables framed by replicas of old-fashioned streetlights while furthest away from her was a bar that sat in front of the expansive steps that lead to the mansion.

Bonner came by her side and placed a hand on her lower back. He leaned his mouth close to her ear. "You were incredible. I'm sure everyone feels good about attending tonight."

Ella turned his direction and opened her mouth to say something, but a line was already forming. Still, she didn't have to force a smile when facing the guests. She extended her hand to the first woman in line.

"Hello, I'm Joan." The woman took Ella's hand. "This is my husband, Milt. We just wanted to thank you for all the wonderful work you're doing."

Ella gave the woman's hand a squeeze. "It's my pleasure, really. Everyone at SecondHope thanks you for all the support."

The personal meetings continued in a similar way until an older gentleman with a familiar face was next in line. He accepted Ella's extended hand and placed another on top of it. "Hello, Ella. Your presentation was impressive. You know, for a bit, you reminded me so much of Josephine."

Ella swallowed. Her mouth had turned dry. "Thank you. I'll take that as a compliment since Josephine was such an amazing person."

"As are you, Ella." The man patted her hand, then released his grip. "You really are a saint."

Sensing her need, Bonner eased away. Ella ended the conversation with the man and felt relieved when Bonner returned with a glass of water. As she raised the glass to her eager lips and mouth, she saw a large instrumental band setting up on the stage. She returned to receiving guests and when the band got close to being ready, the line stopped growing. The last guest drew closer and, in a wave, a sense of exhaustion set into her body and mind. Bonner had remained steadfast in standing next to her and, once the time was appropriate, he encouraged the conversation to end by moving away from the area.

Once they were out of earshot, Ella said, "I could use a minute away. The bar doesn't look crowded. Let's go have a seat."

They navigated to two empty seats at the bar just as the band introduced their first song. Bonner held the barstool for Ella as she got comfortable, then summoned the bartender. Once they were served,

Ella sat in silence, sipping her wine. Bonner leaned close to her and ran his fingers down her arm. "I can't keep my eyes off your bare shoulders," he whispered.

Ella grew a quaint smile and looked his direction. She smoothed the lapel on his jacket. "And you look extra handsome in that tux."

Just as Bonner reached for her hand, a voice interrupted.

"Do you mind if I join you? I need to sit down." Darian sat in the chair on the other side of Ella. He looked across the bar at the bartender, who served him a drink without haste.

Ella kept her sight on Bonner and couldn't resist rolling her eyes.

Bonner leaned back and looked at Darian. "Having a few cocktails tonight?"

Darian picked up the glass and swirled the ice around a few times before taking a drink. "You could say that." He chuckled. With his elbow on the bar, he shifted in their direction. "God! This is great. Isn't it?"

"Yes, lovely." Ella nodded. She examined the green cast around Darian's eyes and her memories as Josephine didn't recall him looking that way. She had a vague sense of seeing someone else that looked like that, but despite her effort, she couldn't piece together the memories.

"Hello everyone." Zofia seemed to appear from nowhere and at the last minute she drew closest to Bonner. "Would you be willing to take a single woman for a dance?"

"Why, of course." Bonner smiled and stood from his chair.

"I just can't wait to get out on the dance floor." Zofia shrugged and slid her arm around Bonner's elbow.

Ella watched them leave but felt stuck in her seat as if something held her there. *Great, now I'm alone with him again.*

"There goes your young escort," Darian said.

She pivoted her head in his direction. "Young escort? What's that supposed to mean?"

He leaned forward on the bar. "It's just he's young, and he waits on you."

"Waits on me?"

"Sure, he holds the chair for you, he gets you what you need, and I'm sure he's not too tired at the end of the day."

Her mouth gaped open. "How could you speak in such a way?"

Darian leaned back in his chair and took another gulp of his drink. "I'm not saying it's a bad thing or anything. Just seems you're going over to the more pleasurable side of things. The other side from dedicating your life to others and all that."

Ella had to work to swallow the wine in her mouth. "Who are you to judge? The crass billionaire who's suddenly interested in doing nice things for his wife." She let out a small cough while covering her mouth with a napkin. "And you know what? To return that artwork would be doing something for someone else. It would be sacrificing an enormous asset."

After a long, hard stare, he let out a belly laugh. "You have such an unexpected edge." His eyes met hers again.

This time, she looked deep into his eyes. With their pupils one-to-one, she could see the brown highlights in his iris. In the vast silence, she sensed the seconds lasted an eternity. Darian leaned closer and slid his hand next to hers. She stared at his hand while he grazed his fingers up and down the back of her hand. His fingertips were electric, and she felt a small quiver inside. Unable to end the interaction right away, she let it go on for a few more seconds before recoiling her hand so it was close to her body.

In response, he sat up straight and returned his focus to his drink. His eyes wandered behind the bar. "Anyway, my returning the artwork wouldn't be such a sacrifice. I owe a lot to the Atrilians." He turned and looked over at the crowd. "Most of my money comes from importing their goods."

Ella raised her eyebrows. "I didn't realize."

Darian furrowed his brow. "Well, sure. Where do you think that wine you're drinking came from?" He gestured his hand toward the dining tables. "Or those linens with the fine stitching? They're Atrilian too."

"And you haven't thought about changing your business practices with the standoff and everything?"

"Why should I?" He grunted. "The Atrilians may have different beliefs, but they aren't terrible people or anything." He shrugged, then produced another hearty laugh. "Now that I think about it, it's absurdly ironic. Your charity event to help the refugees was brought to you by way of the Atrilians." His laughter escalated further.

Ella turned away, trying to ignore how his own words rekindled his laughter. *This man is so infuriating. One minute I want to play handsy with him and the next I want to push him off his bar stool.*

As a pleasant interruption, Ella looked past Darian to see Grace sneaking up on him. Getting near, Grace slid her hand up his shoulder. Then she spoke into his ear, "The music won't last forever." She ran her hand down his arm to grab his hand and give it a light tug. "Do you want to dance with me?"

"A dance with you would be very nice," Darian said, and he let Grace coax him towards the dance floor.

Ella bid the couple farewell and looked around. With perfect timing, Bonner was walking in her direction. She slid off the stool and straightened her dress.

Bonner put out his hand. "Come on, Ella. Let's enjoy a dance before turning in for the night."

Ella's smile grew as she placed her hand in his. "Gladly."

Chapter Fourteen

"When I see the downtown skyline, I feel like I'm home." Ella rested her head on Bonner's shoulder as the train chugged along.

Bonner slid his arm behind her head and leaned closer to the window. "Yah, we'll be back in Dewcall before you know it. I'm glad we took the later train." He tightened his embrace.

Ella let her gaze move along the landscape, anticipating the bend when the train station comes into view. Her stomach did a little dance when she thought about the success of the charity event. She could help so many people with the additional funding, she wasn't sure where to start. Her mind was already back at her desk, preparing her presentation for the board members—which services to expand and others to add. The jerking of the brakes brought her back to the present, and she gathered her things. Bonner led the way out of the train and they weaved through the crowd surrounding the station to arrive at the SecondHope tent.

A few steps past the entrance, Betty, the executive assistant, approached them at a brisk pace. Ella wondered why Betty wasn't at the office and why she was wearing an apron. She felt the corners of her lips getting heavy.

"So glad you're back." Betty took a breath. "Sorry to do this to you since you just arrived, but can you help?" She looked back at the food service area.

"Sure, of course." Ella motioned her hand to encourage Betty forward. "What happened? What do you need?"

"We had a few volunteers who canceled and Chef's righthand person is having minor surgery today, so he's out." Betty started walking towards the back of the tent. "I've been helping Chef, but there isn't anyone to serve the food." Betty waved her hand with a dish towel still in her grasp. "Well, I've been doing both, but…"

"Just tell me what to do." Ella looked back at Bonner. "Will you help too?"

"You don't even have to ask. I'll take our luggage to the van and come back," Bonner said.

Ella followed Betty to the tables where Betty instructed her to work down the line of food: keep the rolls stacked, fill the butter dishes, ladle the stew into bowls, and exchange empty cookie trays with full ones. It seemed simple enough until Ella scanned the line that wrapped around the edges of the tent and trailed out the doorway. She went to work. *Damn. Instead of fooling around in bed all morning, we could have been here earlier.*

Betty took a few steps away and looked over her shoulder. "We'll send Bonner over to help."

Ella pursed her lips as she started ladling stew; the bowls were the shortest in supply. As she did her work, she began smiling at the refugees who came through the line. Soon, she was adding a brief eye contact, a nod, and, once Bonner was helping with the flow, a greeting here and there. While chatting with one gentleman and his family, she noticed the sounds of other conversations coming from the tables.

The noise filled the tent, giving it the feel of a community space.

Things ran with ease, and Ella looked up to check on the length of the line. Her breath came a little easier since it no longer reached outside of the tent. By the entranceway, she noticed a little girl who was about four-years-old. She was just beyond the shadow of the tent, so the sun reflected off her light blonde hair with ringlet curls that skimmed the nape of her neck. The little girl twirled, and her dress whirled around her, making her giggle. Ella's heart lit up like a lightning bug was in her chest. Her sight stayed with the girl as she grabbed a napkin and took a sugar cookie from the tray. She took slow steps towards the girl until she felt a firm hand on her shoulder.

"Ella, no." Bonner nodded towards a group of large men with broad shoulders on the other side of the girl. "I think that's her father. He looks Atrilian and has the traditional tattoo of Jurisha on his arm."

Ella wrinkled her forehead and tugged her shoulder away. Her eyes stared into Bonner's, waiting to see if he would say something more.

"They don't accept handouts of any kind from strangers. It's a pillar of their beliefs that Jurisha and their connection with the land and sea will provide," Bonner said.

"Don't be silly. There's no harm in giving a little girl a cookie." Ella walked away from Bonner, who was standing with his hands on his hips.

Ella held the cookie and bent over near the girl. "My name is Ella. Would you like a cookie?"

The little girl stopped dancing, and her bright blue eyes were wide. She looked back at the group of men and held her fingers to her mouth.

"It's okay, here." Ella held the cookie towards the girl until a shadow of someone approaching blocked the sunshine. A large hand came down and smacked the cookie from Ella's hand. The cookie flew in the air for a short distance before it landed on the concrete and, with a bounce, crumbled into pieces.

"What are you doing?" The voice of the man who approached thundered.

"I was just…" Ella stood up straight.

"Papa, I didn't take the cookie." The little girl cried and hung on to his leg.

The man got closer until he was inches away from Ella's face. Without lowering his volume, he said, "We don't need your kind of charity. What, don't you think I can take care of my child? That you're better than us?"

Ella took a step to the side, edging her way back into the tent. She shook her head. "No, no. It's not that."

"Jurisha will provide." The man looked at her with intense eyes. Then he shifted to the side and leaned over to his crying daughter, knocking his expansive body into Ella.

Ella stumbled backwards with large steps until she fell into a group of folding chairs that were scattered at the end of a table. The chairs slid around her in a ruckus. She placed her hand on the seat of a chair to soften her landing, but as she continued to the ground, a pain ran through her wrist. Before she could orientate herself, Bonner was already helping her to her feet. By then, two police officers had surrounded the man.

Ella held her wrist and tried to intervene. "No, really, it's okay." She leaned into the group.

One of the police officers turned to her attention. "Did he hurt you?"

She looked at her wrist. "No, no. This happened when I fell. It was an accident."

"Are you sure he didn't do that when he hit your hand? We saw it from across the way." The police officer persisted.

Before Ella could answer, the other police officer said, "Let's figure all this out at the station." He put the father in handcuffs as the little girl cried with all her might. "I had a feeling this group would be trouble."

Ella resisted the urge to comfort the child. This was spiraling out of control at a pace she wouldn't have imagined. One police officer led the father away while the other squatted down to the girl's eye level and asked her where her mother was.

"Mama's not here," the girl replied with a sniffle. "Papa. I want Papa." She broke down in tears again and ran in the direction the other officer took her father.

This time, Ella held up her hand as she brushed by the remaining officer. "Let me try." She caught up to the little girl and grabbed her shoulder. Still holding on, Ella kneeled and looked at the girl. "I'm sorry all these scary things have happened, but everything will be alright." She wiped a few tears from the girl's face. "What's your name?"

"My name is Lia."

"That's a lovely name. It's nice to meet you, Lia."

By the time Ella emerged from Dewcall Police Station, it was after sunset and the streetlights were glowing. She held Lia's hand while searching for the SecondHope van, and Frank pulled up to the curb in no time at all. Ella opened the van's side door and encouraged Lia into the furthest seat. Despite her wrist still being sore from her miscalculated landing, she buckled the girl's seatbelt and placed the small suitcase on the van floor. Then, she took the seat next to Lia. "Thank you for picking me up, Frank," she said.

"Sure, and I see we have a visitor." Frank looked over his shoulder for traffic before pulling out onto the street.

Not wanting to upset Lia any further, Ella explained to him in broad brush strokes about what happened and that Lia was staying with her for a short time.

Showing she was paying attention, Lia burst into the end of the conversation. "I'll see Papa soon, and Mama will be here, too," she said and nestled her stuffed rabbit with long ears and dangling legs closer to her.

"That's right," Ella said.

Away from the edge of the downtown, Frank guided the van around a corner. "I asked Bonner to come with but he said he couldn't."

Ella shifted in her seat. "I understand." The sound of a car horn honking in the distance intruded the space. "It's probably better that way. He doesn't know how everything turned out." She looked at Lia, who was nodding off.

The ride remained silent until Frank pulled up to the steps at SecondHope. He parked the van and walked around to assist Ella with the suitcase. Lia, now mostly asleep, needed prodding to get her out of the van, where Ella picked her up and carried her into the building.

"Here, let me take her," Frank said. "It's a long way upstairs."

Ella shifted Lia into Frank's arms. With ease, he took on the girl's weight without setting down the suitcase.

At the top of the steps, Ella unlocked and opened the door to the apartment. She walked in and looked around. "Put her in my bed. I'll sleep on the couch."

Frank stopped with the girl still sleeping on his shoulder. "Grab some linens. She'll be fine on the couch." He swiveled to look at Ella. "You need your sleep."

Ella stared at him for a count of the clock before saying, "I guess you're right." She went to a nearby closet, where she pulled out a set of sheets and a blanket. She set up a bed on the couch and Frank laid Lia down, resting her little head on a pillow.

"Thank you so much." Ella walked Frank to the door. "I'll get her pajamas on and get to bed myself." She rubbed her forehead.

"Alright." Frank put his hand on the doorframe. "I'll be back tomorrow morning. Let me know if you need anything."

"Yes, of course." Ella contemplated how Frank was a man of few words before she closed the door behind him. Then she returned to tucking Lia in by opening the suitcase. A few children's books slid from the top of the clothes inside. She dug around until she found a soft cotton nightgown. With a gentleness she didn't know she had, she undressed Lia and pulled the nightgown over the girl's head. Once they were finished, Ella covered her with the second sheet and a blanket.

Lia shifted and held her bunny tight against her chest. Her eyes opened halfway. "Sing me a song," she said.

Ella settled on the chair close to the couch and leaned in Lia's direction. "A song? I'm not very good at singing."

"But Papa sings to me every night."

"How about I read you a story?" Ella picked up a book that had escaped from the suitcase. "Here's *Bunny Finds a New Friend*." She opened the book and read out loud with animated tones. Before she reached the end, she noticed Lia's breathing had fallen into a rhythmic pattern again, telling her the girl was fast asleep.

Ella kept the silence while she set the book down and walked to her own bed. She fell into the mattress's familiar comfort and pulled the covers up to her shoulders. It wasn't long before her own rhythmic breathing took over and she fell into a deep sleep.

In her mind, a dream took hold. She was standing at the observation area in the park, surrounded by mountains. Fluffy snowflakes drifted to the ground, and on the other side of her, a shadow of a man continued down one of the hiking trails. Returning her gaze to the mountains, she noticed the snowflakes had stopped falling. The sun shone from the sky growing brighter and warmer until the snow was melting. She ran towards the wooded area, fell to her knees in the mud, and scooped a handful of snow from what remained of a snow mound. She stared at the melting snow in her hands and felt each drop of water slide through her fingers.

She awoke with deep spontaneous breaths accompanied by dampness surrounding her neckline. A feeling of emptiness threatened to stay with her so she tossed back the covers and sat up on the side of the bed. It was still dark outside, too early to rise for the day. She thought about Lia sleeping peacefully in the other room, then willed herself to lie back down. With her head stuffed into the pillow, she stared at the dim light coming in through a crack in between two window blinds. She wondered how she could give that little girl back to that brutish man who calls himself a father and if there was anything she could do about it.

Chapter Fifteen

Ella walked Lia down the stairs from the apartment to SecondHope's kitchen. She gathered them breakfast before getting settled at a table in the common area. Looking across the table, she saw Lia was happy with her cereal, scooping in large bites without hesitation. Ella nibbled her toast but couldn't get the morning out of her mind remembering how she helped Lia get ready, brushed her soft curly hair, and tied her small shoes. In all the lifetimes she remembered, she had never been the motherly type, but something about this felt different.

Lia finished every bit of her cereal and let her spoon rest in the bowl. She looked at Ella. "Is it time to see Papa now? Can we go?"

Ella let out a breath. "No, not yet. We will soon." She took Lia's bowl and put it on her own tray. "Why don't you go play with the other kids?"

Lia looked over to the play area with interest, eyeing the children who were laughing and racing around a brightly colored plastic slide. She squirmed in her seat before returning her huge eyes in Ella's direction.

"I'll take you over to meet them." Ella leaned over the table and grew a reassuring smile.

"There." Lia pointed behind Ella.

Ella turned to see Bonner and his stepsister, Olivia, approaching. Ella's thoughts turned inward, but she kept an outward smile. *He isn't going to like this in the least bit, and you know it.*

"Good morning." Bonner placed a hand on the back of Ella's chair. "Who do we have here?"

Ella introduced Lia to everyone, and Lia seemed fond of Olivia. Lia chattered to Olivia about wanting to play with the children and, with encouragement, the two left for the play area.

"So, you want to fill me in?" Bonner's eyesight met Ella's.

"Well, it was a long day yesterday. I didn't press any charges, but since the officers saw part of the incident, they kept Lia's father on a twenty-four-hour hold for disorderly conduct or something along those lines." She leaned her head on her hand, trying to remember the details.

Bonner widened his eyes and raised his eyebrows. "So, you brought her here?"

Ella lifted her head back in his direction. "What was I supposed to do? Let them put her into a foster care facility at that hour?" She leaned back in the chair. "Her mother isn't supposed to be in until later today. And besides, maybe I can do something about her not going back to that home. I mean, the way he—"

Without hesitation, Bonner leapt into her words. "I warned you, Ella, but you didn't listen. The Jurishist take their beliefs seriously."

"Yes, but a father shouldn't behave that way. Besides, I could provide so much more for her."

"You could provide?" Bonner leaned over the table and lowered his voice. "You can't be thinking about interfering with that family. How would that make things better off?" He leaned back and crossed his arms with a piercing look in his eyes. "You know,

I think that all the compliments and all the talk of you being a saint are affecting your reasoning."

"How dare you say I'm irrational?" Ella was partway out of her seat when Frank walked by them, his eyes on the community television.

Without stopping, Frank said, "Come on. The Chancellor from Atril is supposed to make a statement."

With larger concerns to push the argument aside, Ella and Bonner followed Frank to join the group around the community television. Standing up from his seat, a man raised the volume so they could hear the news report over the sounds of children playing on the other side of the room. The words *Breaking News* flashed across the screen, then the Era News desk was revealed. This time, a man with dark hair in an immaculate suit ran the broadcast.

"Hello, I'm John Ruskin, filling in for Andrea Saban, who is out in the field today. Chancellor Kerrell from Atril is about to release a statement. We have them live in the press room at the Atrilian capital, and there seems to be some activity."

The screen flashed to a large, ornate press room where the Chancellor walked out of a side door followed by two other official looking people. The Chancellor took his place at the podium. He kept his eyes down and straightened his dark navy-blue double-breasted suit jacket before looking into the cameras and speaking. "I come to you as a representative of the Atrilian people. As you know, we have surrounded the capital of Treaton. And what I want to make clear is we don't want to harm anyone in the capital. We will also maintain the safe corridor on the west side of the city and citizens are free to come and go as they please." With fingers relaxed, he raised his hands to the level of his shoulders. "Our only interest is to hold the Treatonian troops surrounding the capital in place."

The Chancellor lowered his hands and shifted his weight from one foot to the other, then took a firm stance. "As I speak, additional Atrilian troops are heading south to the city of Ecrad." He looked down for a momentary pause. "The millennial anniversary commemorating when the sea brought the Atrilian's to the land of Ecrad will soon be upon us. And we, as a people, are determined to celebrate our anniversary in our sacred city." He scanned the row of reporters and returned his eyes to the cameras. "Ecrad is the city our lineage built with their bare hands and is rightfully ours. It's our home." He remained motionless for a couple of long seconds, then leaned his body forward in a stiff nod and turned away from the podium. Reporters shouted questions with desperation, yet the Chancellor didn't falter as he left through the same door he entered.

The scene cut to the newsroom, where John was tidying up a stack of papers that he placed on the desk. "It seems the Chancellor kept his message short and to the point. As many predicted, the Atrilian's sole interest lies in the port city of Ecrad." The reporter put a hand over his earpiece and nodded. "Now, we take you to an evolving situation at the Dewcall Train Station. Andrea, can you tell us what's happening?"

The camera went live to show Andrea Saban standing next to another woman who was wiping the remnants of tears from her face.

The reporter looked at the camera. "Sure, John. I'm standing here with Maren Behmen. She is from Treaton and her husband is from Atril. Together, they live in the city of Ecrad." She turned towards the woman. "Maren, can you tell everyone more about your situation?"

"Yes." Maren pulled her sweater tight around her amble body. "I just arrived, and I expected my husband to be here, but my uncle came to pick me up." She sucked in a breath. "He told me something happened yesterday, and the police arrested my husband." Her eyes filled with tears again. "He's a good man and has never been in trouble before. He wanted us to come here to be safe and I just don't understand." She covered her mouth for a moment. "They also have my daughter. And I don't know where she is…"

"Can you tell us your daughter's name?" the reporter asked, encouraging Maren to keep speaking.

"Her name is Lia. She's my baby girl."

With the sound of her name coming over the speaker, Lia's ears must have tuned into the voice. In an instant, she ran across the room. "Mama! Mama!" she cried.

Ella swooped Lia up and swayed back and forth. "It's okay." She pointed at the television. "Your Mama says she loves you." Ella softened the emotion behind the mother's words. "And see, she's going to see you soon."

Lia laid her head on Ella's shoulder. "Mama," Lia whimpered.

Ella stayed in motion, swaying back and forth as she heard the reporter's closing remarks.

"Let's hope the war doesn't divide any more families. Back to you, John."

With a lump in her throat, Ella also remembered when Lia said her Papa sang to her every night. She accepted Bonner was right; she felt Lia's distress and didn't want her to face more harm. The girl had to go back to her parents and, even more so, that is where she belonged. She patted Lia's shoulder. *But why, all the sudden, does it feel like the greater sacrifice to let her go?*

Ella calmed Lia's cries by convincing her it was time to get ready to see her mama and papa. After the news broadcast, she was sure the Dewcall Police Department would be eager to resolve the situation. She took the girl upstairs and together they packed Lia's things in the suitcase, except for her jacket and stuffed rabbit. They had almost finished when someone knocked on her door.

Ella found Betty standing in the hallway. "The officers will be here to pick up Lia in about half an hour," Betty said.

"Pick her up? I thought we were going to the station." Ella hung on to the edge of the door.

"They said something about it being better. There will be a press conference with the family being reunited."

"I see." Ella looked back at Lia, who was humming and making the rabbit dance on her suitcase like it was a stage. "We'll be down in a minute." She turned back in Betty's direction but avoided eye contact. "Thank you."

"You're welcome." Betty retreated down the steps.

Ella sat on the couch close to Lia. "Honey, it's almost time to go. But let me tell you something first."

Lia stopped playing with her bunny and let her lower lip stick out. "Okay, but we're going to where Mama and Papa are, right?"

"Yes, you're going, but I can't go with you. You and bunny will have to be brave for a little while. Two very nice police officers will pick you up and there's no reason to be afraid. Okay?"

Lia snorted and pulled her bunny closer. "I guess." She sat for a moment. "Yes, that will be okay."

Ella felt the lump return to her throat again. "Your parents are going to be very happy to see you." She stood up and gathered the suitcase. "Let's go downstairs."

Lia hung onto her toy and took her jacket. She used the jacket to wrap the bunny as they walked out of the apartment. "Bunny, I'll protect you and keep you warm," she said.

Ella sat with Lia next to the security station where there was a clear view of the main entrance. It wasn't long before a car pulled up in front of the building. They walked towards the door. Each step seemed to take an eternity, yet the end was coming closer.

Outside, two officers, one in uniform and the other in plain clothes, met them at the bottom of the stairs. She recognized the officer in plain clothes from the investigation yesterday.

The officer and Ella exchanged greetings, and he thanked her for taking care of Lia before he leaned over to the girl's eye level. "Hello, Lia, do you remember me?"

Lia nodded her head but tried to hide behind Ella's leg.

Ella put a hand on Lia's shoulder. "It's alright. He's going to take you to your parents."

Lia looked up at her with large, wondering eyes.

"Here, hold my hand." Ella guided the girl to the unmarked police car and opened the door. She helped Lia get settled into the seat, then whispered, "You are so brave." She brushed the girl's hair away from her face. "Goodbye, Lia. I'm glad I got to know you."

As Ella pulled back, Lia waved and said, "Bye, Lady Ella."

"Lady Ella?" Ella laughed while her eyes teared up. "You're going to be just fine." She waved back and closed the car door with a gentle thud.

Now, in the driver's seat, the plain clothes officer gave her a nod and pulled away from the building. Ella watched until the car was out of sight. After a quick pivot, she looked at the ground and gave the bottom step of the stairs a light kick. Then, with a deep breath and a slow exhale, she climbed the stairs while focused on the entrance to SecondHope. She walked inside the threshold and closed the door.

Chapter Sixteen

Inside the doors of SecondHope, Ella noticed Bonner at the security station. He stood up, and he was standing just in the right position so she couldn't escape to her apartment. She approached him at a slow speed. In the absence of true privacy, they exchanged niceties about how they were doing but said nothing that mattered. She looked past him towards the stairwell. *You took him to the charity event; you can hardly deny him your bedroom now.*

"Do you want to come up? I can make us some nighttime tea," she said.

He glanced over his shoulder. "Sure. I mean, if it's fine with you."

Ella led the way up the stairs and into the apartment. The bedding was still on the couch from Lia's visit. Bonner seemed to pay no mind to the condition of the room and went straight to the narrow kitchen. She hesitated a second before pulling up the sheets and blanket. Then she lumped them into a pile onto the window seat in the small dining area. Bonner must have found the teapot on the stove because she heard him filling it with water. By the time she walked into the kitchen, he had placed the teapot back on the stove and was turning up the dial. She opened a cupboard. From its depths, she pulled out two mugs and a box of herbal tea that she slid in his direction. Ella leaned on the counter and rubbed her forehead. Bonner came closer and took her into his arms. In response, her hands slid around his neck with ease.

"This has been difficult for you," he said and kept her close.

"Difficult?" She pulled away from him. "Yes, it's been difficult. What if he's right?"

"Who's right?" Creases on Bonner's forehead appeared.

"Lia's father." Ella groaned and walked back into the living room. "Maybe I do think I'm better than them. I mean, I thought I could do more for Lia." She leaned forward in his direction and placed her hands on her hips. "Maybe you're right. Right that I let the saint comments go to my head."

"I shouldn't have said what I did and I'm sorry." Bonner leaned his hand on the threshold to the kitchen.

"Why shouldn't you?" She spun around, her arms in the air. "I have a luxurious condo just minutes away. But I stay here." She looked at him again. "I have more than enough money. I could do whatever I want. But the money just sits there. Who am I to pretend to be some impoverished martyr?"

"So what? You misgauged the situation. SecondHope is part of who you are and you can't tell me you didn't make mistakes getting here."

"Of course I did, and I learned from them all." She plopped down on the couch. "This was different because I realized something. Something bigger."

"What?" Bonner walked over and sat next to her. His arm found its way behind her shoulders. "You can tell me."

"From the beginning, I was so drawn to Lia, but in the end, I knew letting her go was the bigger sacrifice. That instead of giving her what I thought she needed, there was something better I could give her by guiding her back to her parents."

"Oh, Ella." He pulled her closer and used his hand to raise her chin. "You know there are other ways of giving, even if you forgot about them for a while." He leaned in and kissed her lips until the teapot whistled. Without rushing, he let their lips part and returned to the kitchen. She could hear the noise of the teapot thumping on different surfaces and mugs shifting around on the counter until Bonner appeared with two mugs. He set one in front of Ella before getting comfortable next to her on the couch.

After bobbing her tea bag, Ella lifted her cup and took a premature sip. "So, what about you? Did the news about the Atrilians and the capital in Treaton clear up your plans?"

"I don't know yet." He dipped the tea bag in and out of the water a few more times. "I have to wait to hear back from relatives in Mightwell." He shrugged. "My mother's sister has a farm north of the city, closer to the mountains. If things work out, Mom and Olivia could stay there."

"A farm close to the mountains sounds wonderful." Ella closed her eyes, imagining the scene.

"Yes, and it would be a stable place for them to live." Bonner took a sip of tea from his mug. "Things could happen fast."

Ella leaned back on the couch cushions. "Tell me about Treaton. What's it like living in Mightwell?" As Bonner talked, she sat and listened, asking questions here and there, but for the most part she tried to put together the experiences with the person who was sitting in front of her today. They talked into the early morning hours. Eyes blurry, Bonner raised from the couch. "It's time for me to go."

"Don't go." Ella stood up next to him and put out her hand. "We may only have a few nights left. You're sleeping with me tonight." And that was the same thing she said the next night. And the night after that one, she knew it would be their last night together.

"The time has come. I had to let Lia go and now you, too." Tilting her head with a frown, Ella abandoned worries that someone might see them together near the service entrance. "The last couple of days went by too quick." She grabbed Bonner's hand and rubbed her thumb back and forth on his skin.

He ran his free hand up the side of her face. "It has been wonderful, but the tensions have eased in Mightwell. My mother and stepsister will be safe outside the city, and I must return to the rest of my family."

"I know. You told me." She leaned into his hand with her shoulder and head.

"You are hard to leave." He ran his thumb across her cheek. "But, my snowflake, it seems our time is up." His lips drew in, and Ella absorbed the sensation of his kiss. The feel of his soft lips enclosing hers, the draw to pull him closer, the ache inside for something more.

They released the kiss, and Bonner looked deep into her eyes. "Being with you has been something special."

Ella drew her own smile. "Yes. I wish I could make you understand, but I felt things that I never—"

Bonner wrapped her in his arms, cutting off her words. "I know." He kissed the side of her head. "I know," he said again and held her tight.

She used a hand to pull one of his arms down and leaned back so they could look at one another. "I think it's changed me. The way you made me feel." She rubbed his arm. "Even during difficult times, I somehow feel more centered, more content."

He leaned in closer so his lips were in danger of brushing hers. "Yes, me too. It's a wonderful thing."

Leaning in, she met his lips one last time. They pulled back from the kiss to hug so tight it felt like they were one body. Both unwilling to let go of the embrace, they teetered from side to side for a few beats.

Ella was the first to loosen her hug. "I wish you every blessing, and you're always welcome here." She half smiled.

"You will always be a part of me." Bonner let go of his embrace.

Ella looked down before letting her hands float to her sides, then she felt him make the first step towards the SecondHope Van. In it, Frank waited to take Bonner and his family to the train station. She watched Bonner take the next step. And the next. Not able to bear watching him disappear out the door, she turned and went straight to her office. Inside the room, she closed the door and looked around her desk, seeking some solace. Instead, she thought, *To return my sole focus on SecondHope doesn't feel the same anymore.*

Chapter Seventeen

Darian burst into his bedroom at the Whitmore mansion. "Grace? Where's my lovely wife?" He looked around the room, then heard the faucet running in the bathroom. To let the early afternoon sunlight in, he opened the curtains before sitting on the loveseat. When he heard the bathroom door open, he craned his head so he could see Grace. She took a step into the room and shaded her eyes. He noticed her dress was more casual than usual, and her makeup was less than perfect. "I was going to ask if you wanted to have lunch, but first I want to know, is everything alright?"

Grace walked over to the bed and pulled back the covers. "Everything's fine. I just have a terrible headache." She got into the bed. "I took my migraine medication and am going to rest for a while."

Darian went to her side and helped arrange the covers. "I don't like this. It seems sudden."

Grace gave him a small smile. "You know how my migraines go. I'll be fine in a couple of hours."

He examined her face. It was hard to tell what, but something was making his stomach queasy. "Well, alright. I'll come and check on you in a little while."

"That would be nice. Would you close the curtains before you go? The sunlight is so bright."

"Sure." He leaned over and kissed her cheek. "Feel better soon." He patted her shoulder before standing up straight. An urge to stay with her passed through his body before he went to close the curtains.

As the urge passed, he crept out the door and closed it with an easy touch. He didn't notice Henry approaching and almost bumped into him with full force.

"Apologies, sir. I was just delivering the accounting paperwork Ms. Whitmore requested." Henry stood with his formal posture.

"Grace is resting. It can wait." Darian nudged Henry to walk down the hall.

As the two walked down the stairs, Darian told Henry to bring his lunch to the pool. He wanted to eat after finishing his laps. Henry assured him everything would be ready and continued along to the kitchen while Darian headed for the pool house.

In the pool house, Darian changed into his swimsuit and grabbed a fresh towel. The outdoor pool wasn't overly large but roman-shaped and long enough to swim respectable laps. The sunlight reflected off the water and when he waded down the steps into the shallow end, he noticed it was the perfect temperature. He swam with vigor while his body flowed through the water with ease. The heightened sensation of being in tune with everything prompted him to swim a few extra lengths.

Henry had set a table that, between the fine dishes and artfully arranged food, looked appetizing even from a distance.

"Thanks, my good man," Darian chuckled and sat in a seat where an oversized umbrella protected him from the sun.

"Is there anything else you'll be needing?" Henry asked.

Darian let his eyes roam over the table and put his napkin on his lap. "No, this is great." He looked around. The sun remained bright, the pool was immaculate, and the waves on the sea were rolling in at a soothing pace. "It's so damn beautiful out here, isn't it?"

"Yes, sir. Lovely." Henry's cheek flinched with a hint of a smile.

Darian was still reveling in his surroundings as Henry walked away. He took a bite of the Italian sandwich that was sitting on his plate. It was made with fresh focaccia bread and gourmet cured meats. While his chewing blended the flavors in his mouth, he closed his eyes. After he set down the sandwich, his mind put his new life together: living in an ornate mansion surrounded by impeccable grounds, views of the beautiful sea, and the finest food and drink anytime he desires. He popped a homemade potato chip into his mouth. And his wife, his lovely wife. Grace was more than he could've imagined. He started thinking about her smile, the warmth in her voice, and how she kept her kindness despite people haven't always been kind to her. Still thinking of Grace, he went back to eating his lunch and didn't even change back into his regular clothes before going to check on her.

When Darian opened the door to the bedroom, he found the drapes still closed, keeping the sunlight at bay. The air felt heavy. With a light step, he made his way over to the bed where he saw Grace was facing the other direction. He used a soft hand to rub the back of her shoulder, then spoke into her ear. "You've been resting for a couple of hours. Do you want to get up?" She let out a little mumble but didn't move.

"Grace?" He pulled her shoulder towards him. Her face was pale and the defining wrinkles on it seemed more pronounced than usual. As he rolled her onto her back, she didn't respond.

"Shit. Grace, wake up." He shook the pillow. There was no change. His breathing escalated, and he ran to the other side of the bed. With a shaking hand, he hit the talk button on the intercom. His voice sounded thick when he yelled into the speaker. "Call an ambulance, now,"

A female voice responded. "What has happened?"

"You call a god damned ambulance, now." He resisted an instinct to pound on the intercom instead of giving an answer. "Grace had a headache. Now she's unconscious and I can't wake her."

"Yes sir, I'm dialing as we speak."

Darian ran back over to Grace's side and held her hand. He took a deep breath and sat next to her on the bed. "Hang in here with me." He stroked her hand. "You know what's funny? Now it's me who doesn't know what I would do without you." While he laughed, tears built up in his eyes. "I can't run the mansion without you. And besides, what are we going to do with all that artwork?" He felt her fingers tighten, and he did his best to keep talking to her until the paramedics arrived.

Chapter Eighteen

As Zofia approached the emergency entrance at the hospital, the sliding double doors opened. The air whooshed around and her eyes adjusted to the indoor lighting. She walked into the depths of the waiting area and saw Henry, who gave her a wave. A gentleman was sitting next to Henry, and it turned out to be Officer Dusky. She had met him while he was working security at the Whitmore's charity party and they had a delightful conversation. She joined the group while balancing a tray in her hand.

"I brought coffee and some drinks." She raised the tray before setting it on the side table next to Henry. Then she produced bottles of water and cold tea from her large handbag.

Henry was reluctant but took a bottle of tea. After a long drink, he thanked Zofia for her thoughtfulness. Then, he said, "I wasn't sure if I should contact you. But, since Josephine died, Ms. Whitmore didn't seem to have many people around who she was really close to." He stared off into space.

"I'm glad you did." Zofia picked up the tray again, and with smooth intuition held it so Dusky could help himself to a cup of coffee. She waited while he also took a packet of sugar and a stir stick. She took the remaining coffee for herself and settled into a chair across from the two men.

Henry looked in her direction. "She mentioned you did a reading for her, and she seemed quite happy." He smiled at the memory. "I'm sure she appreciated it."

"That's wonderful to hear. And you've worked with her for many years. You probably know her better than any of us." Zofia sipped her coffee and looked over the rim at Dusky.

"I was on patrol and heard the ambulance call." Officer Dusky looked to the doors that led to the emergency room. "I stopped by to see how she's doing, but there's been no news yet."

"And Darian. Where is he?" Zofia asked.

"The doctor called him back right away, but that was a good half hour, maybe an hour ago." Henry pulled into his thoughts, staring off into space again.

Dusky managed to fill the void. "You know, Zofia, after my wife died, my brother insisted I see this medium he was into. I was having such a bad time and all." He met her eyes. "What she said and how she went about everything, it really helped. I've been curious about mediums ever since."

"I'm sorry you lost your wife, but I'm glad you found comfort." Zofia gave him a warm smile.

"Thanks. It's been a long time now." The two-way radio strapped to his waist came to life with a woman's voice that conveyed a message only Dusky seemed to understand. He stood from his chair. "Damn kids," he mumbled. He conveyed his apologies to Henry and looked at Zofia. "It was nice to see you again."

"Likewise. Would you like me to call you later? Let you know how Grace is doing?"

"Actually, yes." He grabbed the empty sugar packet and used the pen from his chest pocket to write his number down. He handed her the slip. "I wish I was giving you my number under different circumstances."

Zofia accepted the paper. "Maybe we can make up for that another time." She slipped the paper in a side pocket of her handbag for safe keeping.

"I would like that." He stood straight and offered a last goodbye before going on his way.

Zofia looked at Henry, who was flipping through a magazine. *Well, at least he's focused on something.*

She moved her sight to the television across the room and sat with Henry in silence as another half an hour passed. A nurse came out of the emergency room area and told them they could go back to visit Mrs. Whitmore for a short time. As they walked into the ER room, the nurse further explained that they were moving her to the intensive care unit and Mr. Whitmore was meeting with the doctors. The words *intensive care unit* echoed through Zofia's mind and she asked about Grace's condition. The nurse explained in a well-rehearsed manner that Ms. Whitmore was resting comfortably and had been in and out of consciousness. They reached the edge of the curtain, and the nurse went on her way.

"Henry, you go in first. I'll wait out here," Zofia said.

"I'd rather you come with me." Henry shook his head back and forth, then met her eyes. "I haven't been in a situation like this before."

"Alright, we'll go together and I'll hang back for a moment," Zofia whispered. She placed a comforting hand on his arm and walked with him past the semi-open curtain. With her attention focused on Henry,

Zofia had missed the obvious. Grace was lying on her back with her head slightly raised by the incline of the hospital bed. It wasn't what Zofia expected, but there it was, a streak of white light that radiated from the top of Grace's head to the ceiling. As a medium, she understood that light continued past the ceiling, past the confines of the hospital, and past this world until it reached into the other realm. It was a gateway to The Origin. Sometimes the gateway could be seen and sometimes not, but, according to what Zofia knew, Grace was what the people at the hospital called actively dying.

Chapter Nineteen

Darian waited with the ER doctor and nurse sitting across the table. The doctor told him Grace had suffered a ruptured aneurysm, and the prognosis sounded grim, but Darian held on to hope while they waited for the neurologist.

Everyone at the table shifted when a woman in a long white coat walked into the room. The clinicians greeted one another, and the woman joined them at the table.

"I'm Doctor Ritterfield, the ER neurologist." She situated in her chair and placed her hands on the table. "I understand the other doctor has filled you in on your wife's condition. I also have reviewed all the test results and spoke with Grace a little." She paused, the room already thick with sorrow. "And I'm sorry, the surgery for an aneurysm is very risky and, given the size and location of the rupture, it isn't an option. It may be difficult to hear, but the odds are she won't make it through the night."

"Just like that? Isn't there anything that can be done?" Darian looked around the table, then ran his hand through his hair. "You know, this hospital could use a new wing. It would be a great way to repay my gratitude if you would get to work and find a treatment for my wife instead of sitting around talking to me." He banged his fist on the table. Silence filled the room as Darian processed his emotions. His eyes moved from person to person, searching for a different answer, but their faces all confirmed what the doctor had just said. A breath coming from his mouth betrayed him and turned into a gasp. He used his hand to pinch his temples and gasped again, a few tears falling onto the meeting room table.

Dr. Ritterfield leaned over and placed a hand close to Darian. "What I suggest you do is take a minute to yourself, then go spend time with your wife." The neurologist rose from her chair and left the room.

The nurse walked over to a mini refrigerator and produced a bottle of water. She stood behind Darian and placed the water in front of him. "We're sorry how difficult this must be for you. Here, drinking water will help you feel better." A few steps away, she said, "We'll check on your wife's transfer to the ICU and let you know when she's ready for visitors." The nurse continued out the door, followed by the ER doctor.

Alone in the room, Darian opened the water bottle, his head still hanging low. He raised the bottle to his lips and drank half of it down. He took deep breaths until he was ready to get up from his chair. Willing himself to find strength, he wandered around the room a few times. Then he went into the adjoining bathroom and threw cold water on his face. He looked in the mirror and straightened his hair. *You've got to see this one through. No other choice. Keep yourself together.*

Back at the table, he finished drinking the water and threw the empty bottle into the trash bin. He was stretching his back when the nurse returned. She said that Grace was ready for visitors and offered to take him upstairs.

When the elevator doors opened, a nurse from the ICU was already waiting for them. "You must be Mr.

Whitmore." The ICU nurse took a step closer. After Darian introduced himself, the new nurse led him down the hall. She looked at him and said, "She's been asking for you. Right down this way."

At the doorway, the nurse closed the conversation without hesitation. "We put on some music Grace requested, and we'll be monitoring her condition from the nurses' station. Just use the call button if you need anything."

Darian walked into the hospital room, the lights were dimmed and the sound of soft classical music filled the air. The bed was inclined, so Grace was in a partial sitting position and Darian slid the visitor's chair as close as possible to her before sitting down.

Grace produced a close-lipped smile. "There you are. Where have you been?" Her words were strong, but her voice was dry and soft.

"I've been here. I'm here." He picked up her hand and sandwiched it between both his hands. "You know, them damn doctors."

Her smile grew a bit. "I know." She took a labored breath. "I just had this wonderful dream. In it, all these people I knew were surrounded by lush gardens. It reminded me of our conservatory, but it was magical. The sunlight reflected off tiny water droplets that had settled onto the leaves." She smiled again. "My parents were there. And Jonathan was there, too. They were all happy and seemed to be waiting for me."

Darian fought the tightness building in his throat. "That does sound beautiful."

"And thinking of other beautiful things, wasn't the charity event beautiful?" She closed her eyes for a few seconds as if she was imagining the scene. "The way everything came together. The layout, the lighting, and the decorations. And the way we danced."

"It was great. You created a world out of an empty terrace." He rubbed her hand, using a smooth motion.

"I think it was my most extravagant affair." She took another labored breath. "You know what else I like?"

"What? Tell me." Darian leaned even closer.

"Our lunches on the balcony. The view, the sound of the waves, the smell of the salty breeze." She paused. "Our lunches are where we reunited."

"We sure did. And it's been wonderful. One of the best times of my life." Sill holding her hand in his, he kissed her fingers.

Her smile returned even larger than before. "It's been even more than that to me. To me, it's been a dream come true."

Never letting go of Grace's hand, Darian looked down, watching his tears fall to the floor, helpless to make them stop until they were ready to leave on their own. As soon as he could manage, he looked up at her.

"I'm getting pretty tired." She adjusted a little in the bed. "I think I'll just close my eyes for a minute."

"Sure, you rest." Darian stood partway and pulled up the blanket. "I'll just stay here and hold your hand."

"That would be nice." Grace's voice was barely a whisper. Then she closed her eyes.

Darian held fast to her hand and watched her chest. The breaths stopped and her grip loosened. He looked at the screens monitoring her vitals and saw no activity. He stood and let his head fall onto her chest. The tears returned without mercy. "No, no, no, Grace, you don't understand. You reminded me about what it means to love. You taught me about the pleasure in giving." A groan traveled up the back of his throat until it came out of his mouth. "You can't go. Things will never be the same without you."

Chapter Twenty

"What am I going to do now, Henry?" Darian sat at the table on the bedroom balcony and stared at his scotch on the rocks while the condensation ran down the side of the glass. He scanned the view and his throat hurt. "Grace was my pleasure. None of this matters anymore." He drank down the liquid from the glass.

"Mr. Whitmore, what can I bring you? You have to eat something." Henry stood without moving.

"I don't want anything to eat, damn it." Darian swayed a bit as he met eyes with the attendant. "Wasn't the funeral beautiful?"

"Yes, it was very reminiscent of Ms. Whitmore." Henry moved his eyes away from Darian and shifted the plates of food on the table. Then he stood up in his perfect posture. Without trying, he towered over Darian, who remained sitting. "Can I be straightforward with you, sir?"

"Of course, after you get me a fresh drink." Darian held the glass up to the sunlight. "Look at this, the melting ice has defiled my scotch."

"Yes, of course." With a smooth swoop of his hand, Henry grabbed the glass before Darian could take the last watered-down sip. He set the glass aside but made no motion to get a new one. "Sir, let's look at this logically. It's way past lunchtime and you're still sitting here in your robe for the third day in a row."

Darian looked down. Not only was he still in his robe, but it hung open, revealing his bare chest and stomach. With a little effort, he leaned to each side and gathered the belt that was dangling from the loops on the robe. He pulled the front together and tightened the belt. "There, is that better?"

Henry exposed a growing purse on his lips. "Look, sir. When was the last time you took a shower? You have an early dinner scheduled with Zofia."

"Now you're upping the stakes on me?" Darian chuckled, then his face fell serious. "Zofia? What the hell is she coming here for?"

"If I recall correctly, you two scheduled it just after the funeral. Something about a friendly dinner in the parlor. I think she's worried about you."

"Oh, yes," Darian mumbled. "Seemed like a good idea at the time." He rubbed the stubble that had grown on his face. His mind contemplated that the dinner could be a distraction and Zofia was Grace's friend. It might be comforting, in a strange way, that they both have that in common. "Fine, fine. But I want the finest surf and turf the chef can find for dinner." Darian stood from the chair and walked through the bedroom into the bathroom.

Finished with an extremely long shower and a close shave, Darian returned to the bedroom and found the staff had cleaned the room. He scanned the neatly made bed and knew they put on freshly laundered sheets. Henry must have had them waiting with the best of intentions, but with each passing day, Darian found Grace's scent leaving the room. Pretty soon, he wouldn't even smell her floral soap. Trying not to dwell, he let out a sigh and went to the parlor.

After dinner, Darian walked Zofia to the door. He watched her station wagon pull out of sight before deciding to take a long walk around the mansion. He walked around the side of the building and stopped to stare at the side entrance close to the kitchen. His mind went back to memories of being the caterer. It was the spot where he had come out for a drink with his friend Micka before the anniversary party. He smiled. Micka was right about how he described Mr. Whitmore as being all scrunched up. After Darian thought about how everything wasn't as pleasing without Grace, maybe Micka was also right that being a billionaire isn't all that it's cracked up to be. Maybe it was time to find a new life again.

His mind went through past lives, and he remembered being a surfer riding the waves off the coast. At the peak of that life, he found himself in a sweet spot as a wave formed a perfect barrel. The water surrounded him with a thundering roar as he rode the tube and, for that fleeting moment, he knew perfect connection with the sea and at the same time complete freedom. That scene faded to let a few more memories flicker by, and he wasn't sure what he wanted to do that he hadn't already experienced. It took clear direction to invite the trance that let him shift to another body. His shoulders felt heavy as he continued his walk.

Coming full circle, he let himself in the front entrance of the mansion. By the time he opened the bedroom door, he was so absorbed in thought that he walked past the pile of mail Henry left on the desk. After opening the balcony doors, he sat down in his usual spot on the loveseat, not sure what to do besides stay in his thoughts. His mind shifted back to the dinner with Zofia. It was comforting to be around one of Grace's friends. It gave him the feeling of being closer to Grace, even if it was a passing illusion. With the illusion fading, he put his head in hands and let out a strained moan that sounded bizarre, even to his own ears. He sucked in a breath, then exhaled to help center the emotion.

He leaned back and put his feet up on the coffee table. His ears tuned into the sound of the waves, and he let his muscles soften. After a few more crashes of the waves, he heard Grace's voice in a way that was a whisper in his ear yet a voice in his own mind. She said, "I understand everything now. Stop fretting and go look at the mail."

Darian looked around the room and squeezed the throw pillow by his side. He wondered if he was losing his mind but figured there was only one way to find out; he got up and grabbed the stack of mail. It was a large pile, so he carried it back to the loveseat and got comfortable again. While flipping through the items, he looked for anything that stood out. He lifted a large envelope, and a postcard fluttered to the ground. With a grunt, he leaned over and picked it up. When he did, he immediately flipped it to the illustrated side. It was a picture of artwork that reminded him of the old Atrilian drawing in the attic. With his interest piqued, he looked at the other side and saw it was from Ella. The elegant handwriting read, *Darian, Given the recent peace talks, I made it to Ecrad where I'm visiting my young friend, Lia, and her parents. They have been wonderful guides to the city. We went to an art museum, and I ran across the drawing on the front. Isn't it strikingly similar to the one we looked at? I let everyone go ahead so I could spend some time alone with it. I felt like Grace was with me. Ella.*

"Well, I'll be dammed," Darian said to the empty room. Then he had a vivid memory of Zofia sitting at the table during dinner. She had also brought up the artwork and suggested Ella could help do something with it in Grace's honor. He looked at the picture on the front of the postcard again. While he wasn't sure how he would handle his attraction to Ella, it was no loss to stay in this life and do something with the artwork. He had all the comforts he needed and more. A breeze rushed through the balcony doors that sent the window sheers wafting around. He looked up at the ceiling and hollered, "Okay Grace, the drawing will go back to the Atrilians and our little town of Roseacre will get the best damn art museum in the country."

Chapter Twenty-One

With almost two days of traveling behind her, Ella watched the scenery as the train chugged toward the Dewcall station. After Bonner returned home, she thought about using her money to travel, and it surprised her when the call came from Lia's parents. They said that Lia told them all about staying with Lady Ella and they wondered if she would like to visit. It was a wonderful trip, and she smiled as she remembered the sacred sites in the city. Her smile faded because, as it turned out, she left a day early. The news had reported that peace talks between Treaton and Atril were breaking down. Everyone in the city worried the Atrilian troops would start advancing towards Ecrad again. Then the tension became palpable as the number of Treatonian troops around the city increased and businesses took the first steps to prepare for conflict.

Ella sighed and wondered if the number of refugees coming into Dewcall would increase again. Some people had left to return to the capital, leaving empty beds in the SecondHope dormitory. They would have to make sure they were ready for anything. And early next week was the presentation with the board of directors. She looked forward to returning her focus to SecondHope, even though it had a different meaning for her now.

Following her usual route, she made her way to the tent at the train station while rolling her large suitcase behind her and balancing her carryall bag on her shoulder. The area surrounding the train arrivals didn't seem as busy as it had been in the past. At the tent, the lunch service was well underway. The line remained substantial, but looked like it was moving at a steady pace.

Frank leisurely approached her and said, "You made it," before taking her suitcase.

"I sure did." Ella scanned the inside of the tent some more. "It looks like everything is going well."

"Yah, it's been really smooth today." Frank pulled the suitcase closer to him. "I bet you're ready to get back to work."

"I sure am." She followed Frank to the SecondHope van. "Can we stop at my condo first? I want to drop off my things."

"At your condo?" He put the suitcase in the back and got into the driver's seat. "Sure, I'll take you right there."

The van pulled into the small condo complex with clusters of white side-by-side units set on neatly landscaped grounds. Frank helped Ella with her suitcase as she waved to a neighbor. Opening the door, the previous Ella's condo didn't feel like home just yet. To her, it didn't have the familiar sights and smells that tell you it's your space. She opened the suitcase in the living room and pulled out a well-tailored sweater from the top of the pile. It was a purchase she made during her trip, and she wanted to keep it close. Then she lightened her load by removing some items from the carryall bag. Shortly after, they were back on the road and arrived quickly at the steps of SecondHope.

On their way to Ella's office, Frank said, "The numbers of refugees continued to dip after you left." He waited for her to open the office door. "If it stays that way, we should think about serving the homeless again."

"Yes, it would be wise to think strategically about where we place any new refugees so we can free up a wing." She plopped down in the chair behind the desk while Frank lingered in the doorway.

She shrugged. "But we'll have to see how things go before transitioning. Hopefully, the peace talks will start up again."

"Agreed." He leaned over and grabbed the door handle. "It's good to have you back." He met her eyes and closed the door just enough, leaving it ajar.

Ella dug into the pile of work on the desk. She reviewed the files Betty marked as top priority and worked out a task list. Just as she wrote down the last item, her phone rang. She looked at the extension and knew it was Betty. Her eyes went back to the to-do list as she picked up the handset.

"Welcome back." Betty's voice had a high pitch that vibed with happiness.

"Thanks. It's good to be back." Ella couldn't help but match her tone.

"I have Mr. Whitmore on the line for you."

The silence lingered as Ella's mind went blank. "Uh, yes, of course. Send the call over."

It only took Betty a few seconds to shift the lines. Ella stared at the phone as the first ring escalated, not sure what to expect. On impulse, her hand scooped up the handset again. She answered with her professional greeting, and Darian greeted her in a similar way. His voice sounded more subdued that she remembered.

"I was so sorry to hear about Grace and that I wasn't able to pay my respects," Ella said.

"Yes, thank you." He cleared his throat. "Things haven't been the same."

"I can only imagine." Ella gave herself a moment to process the entire situation. "Is there anything I can do for you?"

"That's why I called. I got your postcard. And I'm putting an artwork collection together in honor of Grace. And, well, my lawyers are working on getting the drawing back to the Atrilians. They also helped me find a couple of experts to go through the other pieces, but it's like they speak another language."

Ella let out a soft laugh. "I know what you mean, especially when you put two of them together."

"Good. Anyway, the plan is to auction off a portion of the artwork. Then we can use those proceeds to finance building an art museum that will house the other pieces."

"Oh, really?" She felt her eyes widen.

"Yes. I need someone to help translate the academic stuff and come at it from a different perspective so this can get done right." He paused. "And I wanted to ask if you would be interested in helping for a couple of weeks or so. Since this is a business thing, I can offer you a contract and reimburse you for any travel expenses."

"Oh, I… I don't know." She twisted the phone cord around her finger. "My first thought is if I agreed to the work, I would want to do it for Grace and to give back to the community." As she continued twisting, the phone cord grew tighter around her finger.

"Fine. We can work that out later, but we'd have a room ready for you at the mansion."

"Thank you, that's generous. But when would you want me to visit? I just got back from Ecrad earlier today. I'll be tied up for a while."

"That's fine. It'll take the art experts time to inventory everything. Think about it and get back to me whenever you're ready."

Ella agreed to get back to him soon, and they shifted to talking about her trip. Then Darian mentioned a few more details about the art project. With the conversation coming to a close, they said their goodbyes, and Ella hung up the phone with a soft touch. She looked across her office, feeling off-kilter. *Wait. Did I just have a pleasant conversation with Darian Whitmore?*

His offer buzzed through her mind, then she thought about the green cast around his eyes. She assumed the tension-filled attraction would return when they were around one another. She walked over to the small window in her office. Her eyes scanned the sky, which was just showing signs of sunset. She wondered what Grace would want her to do. Memories of Grace from her time as Josephine came into her mind. The enjoyable lunches, the shared conversations, the mutual collaboration, and her chest ached. She missed her friend. To finish the short self-exploration, she had memories as Ella. She remembered Grace saying that it would be great to share the artwork with the world. A deep breath came out of her mouth as a hefty sigh. *Fine. I'll go for a short trip and see how it goes. I wanted to travel more, anyway.*

Chapter Twenty-Two

Ella found the Whitmore's driver just outside the confines of the Roseacre train station. The driver took her bags and put them in the trunk while she got settled into the backseat. She pulled out the list of artwork Darian had sent for one last review. The image of the mountain landscape painting by Horace Le Compte that she looked at in the attic was clear in her mind. Her time with Bonner seemed to rekindle her draw to the mountains, and it was the first piece she looked at with Darian. She looked forward to seeing the painting again.

The driver got in the car and looked over his shoulder. "Are we going straight to the estate, ma'am?" he asked.

"Yes, that would be perfect."

"Very well." The driver put the car in drive and pulled into the flow of traffic.

Ella returned her focus to the list. She wanted to be prepared, in hopes that her visit would be smooth and quick.

They reached the mansion, and the driver took care of her bags again. He must have known where to take them, because he walked past Henry, who was standing in the large entrance hall.

"Ms. Turner, how nice to see you again," Henry said. "We have your room prepared. Right this way."

"Thanks, Henry." Ella followed the attendant up the stairs, around the corner, and down the hall. It didn't surprise her to find they put her in the same room she stayed in during the charity event. Walking through the door, she felt comfort in the familiar living area. A small couch faced a desk, while a wooden table with two matching chairs sat closer to the window. Alongside that area was a king-sized bed covered in an elegant golden bedspread that complemented the light-colored walls. As her eyes completed her inspection, she spied fresh linens in the sparkling bathroom.

"Shall I have lunch sent up?"

"No, I'm fine. I ate on the train." Ella took her suitcase and placed it on the ornate luggage stand at the foot of the bed. She opened it and removed her hanging clothes to place them in the closet.

"Very well. Just use the intercom if you change your mind." Henry opened the door to leave. "I'll let Mr. Whitmore know you've arrived."

"They're lucky to have you around here." Ella directed a soft smile in Henry's direction.

"Yes, thank you, ma'am." He closed the door with a gentle click of the latch.

Ella took her personal items into the bathroom and freshened up a bit. Then she picked up her paperwork, wandered back down the hallway, and down the stairs. She wasn't sure where they were working on the artwork project, but she would run into someone soon. After a couple of steps into the entryway, she saw Darian come from one of the main hallways.

"Welcome, welcome." He said, and as he approached Ella, he put out a hand. "Sorry, I didn't make it in time to greet you at the door."

Ella accepted his hand, and they exchanged a light handshake. The greenish cast around his eyes had persisted, and his presence still made something inside of her quiver. "No apologies necessary. Henry took me up to the room, and I had a chance to get comfortable."

"Good. I'm glad." Darian shook his head up and down. "I see you brought the inventory."

"Yes, I can't wait to see more of the artwork." Ella's chest felt full and warm.

"Well, no time like the present." Darian led the way across the entryway and down one of the first floor hallways. "Many of the pieces are in the dining hall. That's where we'll host the auction."

The hallway was as beautiful as she remembered. The marble floors were shiny, and the ferns that flanked the sides were lush. She turned the corner with Darian and looked into the dining hall. A large computer and piles of paperwork were on a few tables in the middle of the room. The artwork was clustered in groups around the edges. They had left the protective covers on the pieces, but they looked tidier than in the attic.

Then Darian said, "As we talked about, some are at the university for additional authentication, and some we're certain, will go into the museum. Those we put back into the attic storage for the time being." He led her to the tables at the center of the room. There, he picked up a packet and handed it to her. "Here are the ones we put in the final catalogue for the auction. If we add anything else, we'll bring them out as bonus items at the end."

Ella accepted the papers and let her eyes roam down the page. It seemed little had changed from the last list she reviewed.

Darian placed his hand on top of her hand that was holding the list. "Now listen, say something if you want to change the list." He released his hand. "Maybe a buyer will be disappointed. So what?" He shrugged. "Let me introduce you to everyone and I'll make it clear you have the last word."

Ella stood alongside Darian as he did exactly as he said. She got to know the two art historians and two enthusiastic college interns. They explained the process and how the artwork was organized in the room. When they got to the cluster that was undecided, Darian grasped her upper arm. "Those are the ones that need a final decision on which to include in the bonus items tomorrow. I want you to look at those first."

She fought a strange urge to turn into him so she could use her free hand to slide around his waist. Despite her effort, she still found herself too close to him when she said, "Of course. I'll make it my first priority."

He stared into her eyes while he let his hand rub down her elbow and forearm before releasing his fingers. "Good," he said. Then he looked to the side and took a step back.

"I'll just get started then." Ella had a feeling deep inside herself. The feeling was vast but pleasurable, one she couldn't quite identify. In a feeble attempt to rectify her emotion, she examined his face, the wrinkles at the creases around his eyes, and the slight curve at the corners of his mouth.

"Let's go over your analysis later." He took a few paces away before he looked back towards her and, for a moment, their eyes met again. "I'll arrange to have dinner in the conservatory if it's alright with you."

"That's fine with me." This time, she balanced her response by saying, "I'll be ready for something to eat by then."

"Then it's all set." He excused himself and left them to continue making sense of the vast amount of artwork.

Just as she would at SecondHope, Ella started with the top priority item by working through each piece of artwork in the undecided group. Each time she lifted a cover with protective gloves on her hands, she felt like it was a privilege to see something so precious. About halfway through, she found the oil on canvas of the mountains that she was thinking about earlier. She looked over at the art historian who was sitting at the computer. "Why is this in here? I thought it was going to the museum."

The historian got up and walked over to Ella. "Oh, yes. We were going to put that in the landscape exhibit, but most of the paintings in that group were part of the restoration project so we eliminated the few that didn't date as far back."

"So why not put it in a time period exhibit?" Ella made deeper eye contact with the art historian.

"We could, but since it's realism, it doesn't bring many new techniques. Not that it isn't a good rendition of a past era." He gazed at the painting. "And, well, given the subject, it has a high market value in this area. It's an excellent piece for auction."

"I see your point." Ella scanned the painting again and warmth grew in her chest. She shook off the feeling. "Thanks. I still have some more to go through."

Ella barely heard what the art historian said to close the conversation before he returned to the computer. She stayed focused on the task at hand. With her review of the undecided pieces complete, she went to the auction list and looked at a few she wanted to assess with more detail. She gathered with the art historians and they went over the final decisions. The time had passed without her notice, and she should leave to meet Darian for dinner. She didn't have many updates for him, but her stomach rumbled, so she left the converted dining hall.

When she walked into the conservatory, the familiar sound of the stone waterfall greeted her ears. The table had been set, but the room was empty. She strolled around the room and admired all the plant life. Outside, the sun was in the last stages of setting and, finding its way through the windows, it gave the room an orange-golden cast. She noticed a large plant with orange and purple blooms and went over to investigate. Leaning over, she examined the exquisite petals that fanned out from the sepal. Darian's voice gave her a start, and she whirled around to face him.

"Glad to see you're here." He walked up to the table. "Come, have a seat." While motioning to Ella, he pulled out a chair.

"Thank you." Ella felt her heartbeat increase as he pushed in the chair. "The Birds of Paradise are lovely."

"I didn't notice they were blooming, but there they are." He took the seat across from Ella and looked around. "I like this room."

"Yes, me too." She removed the linen napkin from the table and placed it on her lap.

Henry approached and served drinks, followed by a classic wedge salad. They started dinner as Ella gave Darian an update on the artwork and that there weren't any major changes.

"Well, that's great. Especially since the auction is tomorrow night." He chuckled. "Nothing like taking things to the last minute."

"Yes, I guess so." Ella felt a blush creep up her cheeks because she would have insisted that everything was set days in advance.

"Well, the college interns will be more than happy to stay up all night making sure the pieces are ready and the room is being turned into an auction hall as we speak." He let out another small chuckle before shifting the conversation. "So, you haven't mentioned Bonner. How are you two doing?"

Ella told him about Bonner returning to Mightwell and that his stepsister and mother were staying with relatives outside of town. Next thing she knew, she was telling him about what happened with Lia at the train station. After Henry brought the main course of chicken Kyiv with vegetables and left them to their dinner, Darian told her about the days after Grace's funeral and how Henry helped to pull him out of his downward spiral. Then he went into detail about his dinner with Zofia and receiving the postcard.

"Sometimes, you never know where life is going to take you." Ella took a bite of a neatly cut chicken. "Zofia is an interesting person."

"She sure is interesting, and I have to admit how she explained things made me feel better." He grunted while he added vegetables to his fork. "Given she and Grace got to know each other, she insisted on being here tomorrow. She's going to help greet and check in buyers." He looked thoughtful as he chewed his bite, then said, "I think she'll be staying in the room next to yours."

Ella expressed her approval about her temporary neighbor and took a drink from her water glass. They continued to have an animated conversation about the details of the auction. In a surprise agreement, they passed on dessert and made their way towards the door. Now, talking about the artworks expected to fetch the largest prices, they moved down the hall at a slow but steady pace.

Outside Ella's door, Darian paused and turned to her. "I'm glad you're here," he said, and placed a hand on her elbow.

"Likewise." She patted his shoulder. They stood eye-to-eye for an indiscernible amount of time before bidding each other goodnight.

Ella went into her room and sat on the sofa. While leaning back in the cushions, she let the memories of the day go through her mind. A smile came as she recalled how much of the conversation at dinner was serious, yet they joked, they laughed, and they had a good time. *Are you sure you came here just to honor Grace? You just had a wonderful dinner with Darian Whitmore.*

She indulged in a soft laugh and went to put on her nightgown. To be ready for whatever tomorrow may bring, the more sleep she got the better.

Chapter Twenty-Three

Darian finished putting on his cufflinks, followed by his tuxedo jacket. He took one last glance in the bedroom mirror at the traditional look he wore, complete with a black button vest and self-tie bow tie. It was unusual for him to feel so nervous. On his way across the room, he took in a deep breath and welcomed the smell of sea air into his senses. He picked up his speech and, despite its short length, he gave the page one last skim. Tucking the paper into his inside breast pocket, he walked out the door, still deep in thought. He turned the corner and saw Ella coming his way. Her silhouette moved with elegance. She had on a black full-length dress that flowed around her legs as she walked. Her eyes flickered with recognition when she saw him, and he couldn't remember seeing her smile grow so large.

He resumed walking, pacing himself just right so they would meet at the top of the staircase. His stomach tightened when he lifted his elbow so she could slide her hand around his arm. He met her eyes. "You look beautiful tonight," he said.

To match her smile, a hint of red creeped into Ella's face. She accepted his arm and looked him over. "And you look very handsome."

He guided her down the stairs. It felt like a grand entrance, even though the guest had just started to arrive. As soon as his foot hit the landing, he could only give her one last glance until the congratulations of guests pulled him away. Out of the corner of his eye, he watched as other guests greeted Ella, many of them remembering her from the charity event. Then he got caught up in the moment, greeting everyone with vigor until Henry tapped him on his shoulder.

"Sir, it's time to get ready for your speech."

"Thank you. Let's go." He walked with Henry, passing the artwork that lined the hallway for viewing. "Now, remember to keep the champagne flowing. I don't care how much we go through."

"Yes, sir. Of course." Henry made the turn towards the kitchen.

As Darian passed the registration desk, a voice called his name. He slowed to see Zofia, who had already resumed chatting with guests and handing out catalogues.

"Zofia. Hello." Once he reached her, he surprised himself and leaned in to peck her cheek. "Thank you for being here."

"My pleasure. I'm sure all of this would make Grace very happy." Zofia inspected his tux and brushed off one of his shoulders. "You have gone all out tonight."

"Well, thank you. When the situation warrants." Darian chuckled.

"That's right." Zofia giggled. "Everything is going to be wonderful."

Darian strode into the dining hall, now turned auction room. They had placed a red velvet backdrop on the ground level stage. That way, artwork could be rolled in on displays from one side of the stage and the display turned to reveal the artwork. Once the sale was finished, it could then be rolled out the other side of the stage and circled back behind the backdrop. After that, it went to a secure room where they would await their new owners.

In front of the stage were neat rows of elegant dining chairs that extended for a good part of the room, while clusters of tables and chairs were arranged behind them. Darian stopped and greeted the auctioneer before stepping into the stage area and nodding to the project manager across the room. With that, the project manager flashed the chandelier lights on and off, telling everyone it was time to get into their seats. Once the chairs were almost full, the project manager adjusted the lights, so the focus was on the stage. Everyone in the audience of buyers hushed.

After an appropriate pause, Darian got behind the podium and smoothed his paper out in front of him.

"Good evening, everyone." He scanned over the crowd. "I think everyone knows me. I'm Darian Whitmore. Thank you for coming and supporting the museum in honor of Grace Whitmore." He let the silence take over for a moment. "As we all know, Grace was a wonderful person. She was honest and kind with a strength that, even on her most challenging days, surprised me. It's my pleasure to create a museum in her honor and, as she wanted, to share the Whitmore artwork with the world." A light applause generated from the audience.

He took a breath, then refocused. "As some of you may have noticed, outside the room are a few prototype drawings for the museum." He gestured towards the door. "If you haven't already, be sure to take a look at them before you leave. We wanted everyone here to be the first to see the plans for what is to come." Another round of applause rippled across the audience. Darian smiled and looked around the room. "Enjoy the auction. Not only do you have the opportunity to obtain a rare piece of artwork, but also to support the community. Thank you." He raised his hand to the side. "I'll keep my words short and turn things over to our auctioneer."

The crowd applauded with vigor as the auctioneer took over the podium with his gavel in hand. The applause ended, and a sense of anticipation filled the room. After going over the ground rules for bidding, the auctioneer said, "Let the auction begin." He raised his gavel and brought it down on the wooden sound block with a bang. He paid no attention to the applause and signaled for the first item. "Here we have Lot 1—"

The voice tapered off as Darian stepped out of the room and let the door close. While taking a moment to himself, he noticed Ella standing by the check-in table talking to Zofia, who was seated on the other side. The two women exchanged conversation, then laughed in unison. Caught up in how captivating Ella can be, he gravitated over to the table.

Ella grew a coy smile. "Zofia was just telling me she's been dating Officer Dusky."

"Oh, really." Darian felt his face brighten. "Dusky's a good guy. He's around here somewhere, helping with security."

"I know." Zofia winked. "I hope to see him later."

The heightening sounds of clapping came from the auction, intruding in on the conversation.

"Did everything get started?" Ella looked at Darian while raising her eyebrows.

"Yes, they've started." He looked back at the door. "Everything seems to be going well."

"It's going very well." Zofia leaned a little over the table. "Why don't you two watch? I'm sure it's going to be exciting."

Ella exchanged a look with Darian. "Let's go. I agree. It would be thrilling to watch."

Darian accompanied Ella into the auction room, and they sat at one of the tables in the back of the room. As the pieces rolled out, the audience applauded, and the energy from vigorous bidding filled the space. The auctioneer kept things moving, while using wit to further stoke the audience's reactions. Then the last two lots in the catalogued collection, the star pieces of the night, got everyone in an escalated state.

"Ladies and gentlemen, we now have a few bonus pieces," announced the auctioneer. The applause rose to another level.

Darian noticed Ella's expression turn downward, and she grabbed his arm, letting her forehead fall onto his shoulder.

"I can't watch," she said.

"What do you mean?" he asked in a high pitch.

"I agreed with the decision, but I can't stand the thought of the next one going into someone's private collection where I'll never see it again." She pushed her forehead deeper into his shoulder.

"What? You like that one?"

"Well, yes. But I'm just caught up in the moment." She pulled away and looked at him.

His eyes still attached to hers, he got out of the seat. With the crowd quieting, the auctioneer motioned the sale forward. Walking in front of the tables, Darian stopped and waved his hands over his head. The porters had spun the artwork stand halfway around, so the painting started to become visible to the buyers. While noticing Darian's bold gesture, the auctioneer signaled the porters to stop, and he took a step away from the podium. The experienced porters spun the display back to where its contents were hidden.

Darian used long strides to get to the next set of porters. He told them to move the next artwork forward, pushing the one already on stage out the other side. Once behind the backdrop, he could hear the auctioneer make a smooth recovery, followed by the audience's reaction to the next item. Darian reached the painting that was just retrieved from sale and looked at the scene of the mountains. His mind worked to tell himself that since Ella was providing her services without pay, it was the right thing to do. That was easier than admitting to himself the deep feelings he harbored for her.

He led the porters to the secure room and told them to guard the painting. Then he found Henry in the kitchen organizing everyone for the clean-up effort to come.

"Henry, I need a favor," Darian called out and watched Henry come to his side.

"Yes, what can I do for you, sir?"

"I need you to take a piece of artwork up to Ella's room and find a place to display it in the living area."

"Of course, I can take care of it." Henry struggled to hold back a smile.

Darian ignored Henry's facial expression and took him to the painting. As directed, the porters were still there, and they went with Henry to take it upstairs. He watched the small group until they were a good way down the hall before returning to the auction.

Ella was still sitting at the table as he slid into his chair. She put her hand on his arm and pulled him closer to her so she could whisper in his ear. "That was incredibly giving, saving that painting for the museum. Thank you."

"If you like anything that much, it's something I would want in my collection." His gaze lingered before they returned to watching the auction. With only a few items left, the event soon came to a close. The buyers clapped, and the applause continued as they stood to their feet. Darian went by the exit and bid farewells as everyone passed. Ella had walked out with him and stood a few feet away, extending well wishes with others. Involved in a conversation, she walked out with a group and out of his sight.

Once the line dwindled, Darian peered into the dining room, where the staff was already stacking chairs and emptying garbage bins. Across the room, a vacuum cleaner hummed to life. He had hoped to get an update about the painting delivery, but there was no sign of Henry.

Darian walked down the hall and up the stairs, feeling empty. The auction was over, and he found himself alone. At the top of the flight, he stood looking down the hallway leading to the guest rooms. He wasn't sure how Ella would receive a knock on her door this late in the evening. He felt a strange tug, as if he was being pulled down the hall, so he moved closer to her door, no longer thinking about his actions. At the door, he stood for many seconds before his hand reached up, made a loose fist, and tapped on the wood. He heard Ella's voice from inside the room, and the door opened a crack. Once she saw him, she flung it wide open.

"I was wondering if you would stop by." She walked into the room and turned back towards him, her pink chiffon robe and nightgown brushing her calves. "I can't believe you had this brought up here." She looked at the painting with her hands at her sides. "It's just here to look at, right? You don't mean for me to have it."

He rubbed his hand over his mouth so the words could come out. "I do mean for you to have it. I wanted to surprise you. It just seemed that you liked it so much it belongs with you."

She looked at him and shook her head. "No, I couldn't accept such a gift."

"You can accept such a gift. Besides, it's one of how many pieces? Take the painting, Ella."

She gazed at the painting. "It would make my condo feel more like home." Her torso turned in his direction. "I haven't done anything like this before but thank you. It's beyond generous."

"I haven't done anything like this before, either." He looked down for a moment before saying, "It's my pleasure."

She clinched her hands in front of her chest and stepped closer to the painting. "It's wonderful."

The sound of a knock on the door came into the room. Her head turned, and her smile never let up. "That must be Henry. With everything going on, I've had nothing to eat since lunch." She opened the door and directed Henry to the small table in the room.

"Here you are ma'am. A variety of hors d'oeuvres," Henry said, while she looked over the contents.

Henry turned to Darian. "Is there anything I can get for you, sir?"

"No, thank you." He moved closer to Henry, nudging the attendant towards the door.

"Very well. Just let me know if you need anything else." Henry made a swift exit.

Ella picked a few items from the trays and put them on a small plate. "These smell incredible. Would you like anything?"

"No, thanks, I'm fine." He held up a hand. "It's been a long day. Do you mind if I remove my tuxedo jacket?"

"Please, make yourself comfortable."

After sliding the jacket off his arms, he tossed it on the side of the couch and, just when he was about to loosen his bow tie, he looked at her. She was sitting at the table using a knife and fork to cut an hors d'oeuvres in half.

His focus became intense, and he watched her every movement.

She lifted one bite with her fingers and looked at him. "Salmon canapés are my favorite," she said.

It was hard for him to move. Some of his last memories as a caterer were clear in his mind and he put it all together.

In tune, she dropped the half salmon canapé back on her plate. Then she stood up and looked him up and down in his black bow tie and vest.

"It's you. You're the old woman." The words came out of his tight throat while the room circled around him.

"It's you. You're the caterer with the green cast around his eyes."

He stepped forward with force. "No, you have the green glistening eyes."

"It couldn't be, could it?" Ella slid her hands up her temples. "You know how to transfer to other bodies? You've lived many lives?" She turned away and an emotive noise escaped from the back of her throat.

Darian used a finger to point at her. "That's how you knew so much about art. You learned it in a previous life." It took a while before he softened his tone and said, "I've never met anyone like me."

It took an equally long time before she turned to face him again. "Before I started SecondHope, I was an art curator at a museum." The tension swirled around her, confusion amplifying in the room. "I haven't met anyone like me either. What do we do now?"

He walked closer to her. "We give into it. We can see who the other truly is. We let ourselves love one another."

Ella seemed to speak her thoughts out loud. "So, you weren't married to Grace for ten years?"

"Not in the least bit. I've only been in this body since just after the anniversary party."

"But you still did all this for her?" She made a broad gesture with her hands. "You still did this for me?" She shifted her gesture to the painting.

Ella paused before making eye contact with him again. She leaned her head to the side. It only took a slight movement until their bodies were almost touching one another. "Is this hand tied?" She answered one last question for herself and tugged at his bow tie until it unraveled. Then she pulled it away from him and tossed it to the side.

Darian swooped one hand around her waist and the other up her cheek. Pulling her as close as he could, his lips met hers. As their kisses turned passionate, electric pulses ran through his body, and he felt a force pushing them closer together. The desire within him was almost maddening. It took all his effort, but he pulled back and looked at her face. He used his fingers to untie the bow at the top of her robe and pulled it away from her shoulders until it fell to the floor.

She leaned into him and kissed his lips. The kisses came fast, creating an instinctive rhythm that heightened their growing passion. He let his hands feel around her shoulders, down to the small of her back, and he tightened his embrace while his kisses wandered down her neck.

Her words came breathless. "I realize now how difficult it was to hold all this back." This time, they joined in a tight kiss with their lips pressed hard against one another.

Overwhelmed with sensation, a flash of when Darian completed his last transfer went through his mind. The feeling that he had to give himself completely came familiar, and he sensed this was something larger than themselves. Without hesitation, he took her hand and lead her closer to the bed. There, he raised her hand and guided her under his arm in a twirl. She completed the three-quarter turn, and he pulled her into his chest. Then he slid one arm below her shoulders and the other behind her knees, lifting her in the air. With her in his arms, he navigated the last few steps and laid her on the bed. Standing straight, he removed his vest and unbuttoned his shirt before giving into the draw to kiss her lips again. He leaned over and let his lips caress hers, light and sensuous at first, but then the never-ending passion returned. Locked in a deep kiss of longing, she slid her body towards the center of the bed, pulling him next to her where they would come together in a bliss that would last an eternity.

Chapter Twenty-Four

Zofia delighted in walking arm and arm with Dusky. "I'm so glad I found you after the auction. Thank you for seeing me to my room." She gave his muscular upper arm a squeeze. "There's something romantic about this old mansion but also something…" Her words stopped while her mind searched for the right way to continue. "Something otherworldly, I guess."

Dusky looked around the large entryway hall before taking the first step up the stairs. "Well, some strange things have happened here."

"That wouldn't surprise me." Zofia giggled, never losing pace with his steps. She thought about Darian and Ella with the spirits caught in their energy fields. She did her best to help the soul hoppers discover one another, and things seemed to be progressing. At the top of the stairs, a gesture of her hand directed Dusky down the hallway.

"Boy, something feels strange." Dusky paused his footsteps. "The hairs on my arms are standing up."

Zofia rubbed his arm with vigor. "I'm sure it's nothing. Maybe it's a chill." She pulled him down the hall, closer to her door. Her mind didn't doubt his officer intuition. She felt it, too, but coming across a bit of energy wasn't so unusual for her, especially in a building with as much history as this one.

In front of the door, Zofia turned to look at Dusky. He leaned closer, and they exchanged a soft kiss, followed by another. She leaned back. "You know, I'm glad we got to see one another tonight."

"I am, too." Dusky smiled.

Zofia felt tender and ran her fingers through his hair. He responded by welcoming another goodnight kiss. As they parted, Zofia felt a distinct wave of lightheadedness that wasn't romantic. She put one hand on the doorframe to steady herself and one on her chest to help her equilibrium return.

"Are you okay?" Dusky moved his head to get a better look at her face. Like a silent explosion, the door next to them burst into pieces while a wind rushed from the room with such force it knocked them to the ground. On hands and knees, Dusky corralled Zofia to the other side of the hallway and covered her body with his. The wind whipped around, throwing up wood dust and tiny splinters from the door. They stayed in the protective position while turning their heads so they could keep their eyes towards the source of the eruption.

Zofia saw multiple spirits still embodying a greenish hue, all flying out the doorway. The spirits bumped around in the hallway before one found a way out through the ceiling. During its exit, it let out a bizarre screech that hurt her ears and echoed in her mind. The sound seemed to catch the other spirits' attention because they followed that one out through the ceiling. Then, if the historical records were correct, they continued their blissful journey all the way back to The Origin.

When the spirits cleared the hallway, the wind calmed, and Zofia pushed Dusky away from her so she could rise to her feet.

In unison, he wobbled to his feet and grabbed her arm. Tight. "Holy shit. Did you see that? Were those ghosts or something?"

"You saw them, too?" She took a step closer to where the door once stood, debris crackling under her feet. Dusky remained close behind her with a hand on each shoulder. She turned her head to the side so she could see him out of the corner of her eye. "If it's what I think happened, they were spirits now freed. We have to find out."

"In all my years on the police force, I've faced many things, but that was terrifying." Dusky held fast to her shoulders. "Still, I should go first." He used his hands to encourage her to stand behind him and, keeping their bodies against one another, they crept towards the door. Everything remained silent, aside from the sound of their slow steps. Getting closer to the entryway, he kicked a few large pieces of wood aside.

Zofia could smell fresh air and figured the windows had been blown out, too. "Be careful of glass," she said.

"Yah, I've got it covered." Leaving Zofia a few steps behind, he moved into the room where evidence of the spirit's release and the wind was everywhere. "Oh, lord." Dusky pulled his two-way radio out of his belt holder. He ran over to the bed while he called for backup and an ambulance.

With Dusky distracted by dispatch, Zofia moved to get a good look at the room. She could see Darian and Ella on the bed, motionless. Despite she knew what had happened, she approached them and looked for telltale signs of breathing. She could find none. She turned away. *Their souls came together through a union of mind and body in a love so intense that it created a powerful force.*

She examined the disheveled room and looked at Dusky, who was tucking the radio back into his belt. "We can't leave them like this," she said.

"Yes, we can." Dusky almost seemed to snicker. "We do nothing but tell the truth. Well, the truth minus the details about those ghost-things." He looked at the ceiling as if he were making sure they were all gone. "It was an unexplained explosion. Where those two are now, they won't care how they're found."

With his words, Zofia further remembered that once they joined, the soul hoppers would return to The Origin and be blessed by becoming one with all things. "You know, I think you're right," Zofia said before walking out of the room.

Chapter Twenty-Five

Zofia looked out the window while finishing a few dishes. The familiar task helped her embrace the relief of Darian and Ella's funerals being over. She liked the peace. She liked the aroma of breakfast foods that were filling her small apartment. Set on the second floor of a house, she could hear footsteps coming up the wooden stairs, followed by a knock on her door. From the kitchen's threshold, she could see Dusky through the diamond-shaped window at the top. "Come on in, sweetheart," she called.

Dusky walked in and approached her. "I like when you call me sweetheart, it's kind of old-fashioned." He kissed her lips, then brought his hands to her shoulders, prolonging the affection.

Zofia giggled and ran her finger down his chest. "I think it's defiantly old-fashioned." After a seductive gaze, she broke away from him and opened the oven. Peering inside, she could see a few soft spots on top of the egg casserole. "Brunch isn't ready yet. Would you like to have a seat on the couch?"

"You know I do." Dusky plopped down on the couch and grabbed the remote from the side table. "You don't mind if I put on my show, do you?"

"Not at all." Zofia walked over and sat down next to him. They chatted until the commercials were finished, then the show started up. *Dressed for Crime* was a hit some years back, but a local station picked it up for syndication and put it in the midmorning spot. Dusky couldn't get enough of it.

"See here? This is the one where Cal finally gets busted." He set the remote down on the side table without taking his eyes off the screen.

Zofia slid her arm behind him and scratched his back. The episode started with a chase scene. Two cars rounded a corner on a dirt road, then the show cut out. The words *Breaking News* ran across the screen.

"What?" Dusky flailed his hands at the television.

Zofia placed a hand on his arm in a way that encouraged him to relax and turned her attention to the report.

The view switched to a reporter sitting at a desk. "Hello, this is Andrea Saban from Era News. We have some recent developments. We're about to go to a press conference with Prime Minister Adamaris from Treaton and Chancellor Kerrell from Atril already in progress. They are together in the city of Ecrad." She shifted some papers across the desk. "Let's find out what they have to say."

The screen flashed to a plain conference room with tan walls. On one side, Lia held her floppy bunny while she stood in between her parents with Prime Minister Adamaris standing closer to the camera. On the other side, Chancellor Kerrell was standing next to the Prime Minister and set further back behind him was a large drawing.

Prime Minister Adamaris stepped forward and spoke first. "It seems our prayers as a community have been heard. It brings me happiness to make this announcement." He glanced at the Chancellor. "It has been an arduous road, but after gaining wisdom from the city of Dewcall, we have agreed that the city of Ecrad will become a shared city between our two countries."

The Prime Minister looked into the cameras and said, "Just behind me are Alex Behmen, his wife Maren, and their daughter Lia." He looked over his shoulder at the group. "Alex is from Atril while Maren is from Treaton. They have faced unwarranted challenges, yet the bond of their family is strong. The love between them is strong." He raised his hand in their direction. "They have been inspiration to us all." With that, Prime Minister Adamaris lowered his head and stepped back.

Chancellor Kerrell stepped forward to speak next. "As a representative of the Atrilian people, I persisted through difficult negations and the city of Ecrad has returned to being part of our home." He nodded at Prime Minister Adamaris. "And, behind me is a drawing that dates back almost one-thousand years. The artwork, once taken from us, has been returned. We express our gratitude to those who were part of seeing it here." He looked back at the drawing for a few seconds. "This drawing depicts the Atrilians building the sacred city. The city where we are now free to celebrate our millennial anniversary. To share our heritage with everyone, the artwork will remain on permanent display in the site that commemorates the sacred energy stone."

The two men met eyes and moved closer to one another. Now, standing side by side, they clasped hands and, in a unified action, raised their hands above their heads. The flashes from the cameras continued even as the scene cut out and returned to the news desk where Andrea Saban sat. She looked

into the camera with a wide smile and watery eyes.
"Well, there you have it. Peace at last."

About the Author

Laura is the author of fiction stories that say something through a twist on reality. Through her tales, she weaves in themes such as raising consciousness, facilitating high vibrational energy, and guiding the soul's journey. She holds a master's degree in philosophy and currently serves as a short story judge. When Laura's not engrossed in the written word, she finds joy in connecting with others, embracing nature, and delving in the depths of various documentaries. To join her on her journey, subscribe to *Laura's Latest* newsletter and find out more at: www.lauraclementzauthor.com

One Final Note

Thank you for reading, *Soul Hoppers*. Reviews mean a lot to authors and other readers. If you enjoyed the book, please take a moment to leave a short review at Amazon.com, and if you are member of the community, at Goodreads.com.